# SHERLOCK HOLMES
# AND THE
# EGYPTIAN HALL
# ADVENTURE

# SHERLOCK HOLMES AND THE EGYPTIAN HALL ADVENTURE

by
Val Andrews

BREESE
BOOKS
LONDON

First published in Great Britain by
Breese Books Ltd
164 Kensington Park Road, London W11 2ER, England

© Val Andrews, 1993

First published in 1994
Reprinted November 1995
Reprinted April 1996
Reprinted May 1997
Reprinted November 1999

ISBN: 0 947533 43 5

Typeset in 11½/13½ Bembo by Ann Buchan (Typesetters), Middlesex
Printed and bound in Great Britain
by Itchen Printers Limited, Southampton

Dedicated to the memory of
that brilliant playwright and screenwriter
Barre Lyndon
(1896–1972).
My thanks go to his son,
Roger Linden,
my good friend
who suggested the subject for this story.
Roger, a professional magician, now resides
near St Louis, Missouri.
As a boy in England he was
the final pupil of
the great
DAVID DEVANT.

Val Andrews – September 1993

# Introduction

J.N. Maskelyne, the conjurer and inventor operated the famous Egyptian Hall in London's West End. It was a theatre of magic and mystery and was run, first in partnership with Alfred Cook and later with David Devant, and in my student days it afforded me many happy hours.

In 1898 my friend Mr Sherlock Holmes became involved in a mystery to rival any created by the conjurers who trod the historic boards there. When Maskelyne moved his enterprise to St George's Hall in 1905 it was never quite the same. But of course by that time Holmes had left Baker Street, and to my mind the metropolis itself had lost much of its entertainment value.

Therefore it gives me particular pleasure to recreate for my readers an episode recalling the days when the conjurer was still in his exotic setting and Sherlock Holmes was still inhabiting 221b Baker Street.

John H. Watson, M.D.
August 1928

# CHAPTER ONE

# The Conjurer's Problem

The year 1898 was a particularly busy and fruitful one for my friend, Mr Sherlock Holmes. I can well remember not only the exhilaration of being allowed to participate in some of his most notable cases, but also my relief that his breakdown of the previous year seemed happily resolved. Once restored to good health, Holmes quickly returned to his old regime of little sleep and intense activity.

It was during that year that Holmes showed his genius had been unimpaired by nervous illness. 'The Adventure of the Dancing Men' and that of 'The Retired Colourman' I have of course recorded and published. But there were other notable cases during that year, some of which I have been unable to present to my readers for reasons of good taste or consideration for the persons involved. Yet I still have unpublished details of one case which presents no such difficulties, and which I feel would interest all of you who have been good enough to express a liking for these narrations of mine. My old files and folders refer to it as 'The Randolph Case', but we, that is Holmes and I, have been more inclined to refer to it as 'The Egyptian Hall Adventure'.

On a recent visit to my dear old friend at his Sussex retreat, I asked his permission to relate the episode. Typically he said, 'Watson, I can think of no reason why you should not but please, I implore you not to ladle on the sauce of sensationalism with which you have often dressed your accounts of my adventures!' If then, this narrative would seem at times to underplay the dramatic, you will have only my friend to blame.

One morning in the late spring of '98 I appeared at breakfast at what was for me an early hour, only to find Sherlock Holmes fully dressed, relishing his second cup of coffee. His alert appearance suggested that for once he had slept for a few hours. He surveyed me with mock-severity.

'Upon my word, Watson, my dear fellow, I believe you rise a fraction of a minute later with each morning.' I grunted some sort of reply and, as I prepared to deal with my devilled kidneys he busied himself, scribbling upon a scrap of paper and chuckling at that which he inscribed. He said, 'According to my calculations, by the fifteenth of July in the year 1901, you will arise at noon, exactly!' Not wishing to encourage levity at such an early hour, I concentrated upon my breakfast, aware however, that my friend was studying me carefully. At length he broke the silence by saying, 'I see that you have no professional calls to make this morning.' It was not a question but rather an assured statement of fact. It was true I was wearing a town suit, hardly of the formal variety required of a doctor. This was, in fact, probably the most obvious deduction I had ever heard my friend make. I said as much and he agreed, adding, 'However, I imagine that you are turned out well enough for a visit to the bookseller?' I started, 'How could you, even given your methods, know I was planning to visit my bookseller rather than, shall we say, my tailor?'

Holmes' keen eyes fairly twinkled as he explained, 'Last evening, when you were sitting reading your book, I noticed that you finished it. I further noted that you searched the advertisements at the back of the book, presumably looking for other titles by the same author. As you ran your finger down the list I saw the change in your expression, doubtless upon finding that which you sought: a title by the same author, one which you had not read.'

I pushed my plate from me, no longer puzzled. After all, I was somewhat used to these seeming mysteries being explained away by deductive logic. I replied, 'As ever you are right Holmes, and it is really very simple when you explain it. But is it not a little early in the day for such brilliant deductions?' Holmes rejoined, 'On the contrary Watson, for a client is to call shortly and I would like you, if you will, to postpone your literary expedition that I might have your valuable support.' I asked, 'At what time is he calling?' Holmes remonstrated, 'With regard to the gender of my client, have I given any indication in what I have said?' I played Holmes at his own game by saying, 'No, but the room is already full of shag-fumes. Even you would have confined your smoking to cigarettes if expecting a lady!'

Holmes clapped his hands in a slow, sardonic applause. 'Excellent Watson! Your hibernation has not dulled your wits. Knowing my methods as you do, apart from the fact that we are expecting a Mr Cyril Randolph, I would appreciate your comments upon this calling card.' He handed me a visiting card which I studied carefully.

The card, which measured about three inches by four, announced simply, 'Mr Cyril Randolph' who had an address in Hampstead. After studying it for about a minute I said, 'It is somewhat larger than the cards used in polite society.' Holmes nodded and passing me his lens, bade me turn the card over. On its reverse side was a neatly written message in ink, 'Will call upon you tomorrow morning at a quarter to ten upon a matter of some urgency.' I noticed a small pink mark or stain at one corner of the card and remarked upon it. 'I suspect that this man is an artist!' Holmes asked 'Why so?' I replied, 'Such a calling would explain both the eccentricity of size and the small trace of oil paint at the corner.'

There was no applause this time, sardonic or otherwise, as Holmes said, 'Your train of thought is interesting if inaccurate. I believe Mr Randolph to be an actor or music-hall performer.' I asked, sharply, 'Would the card not state as much, were that the case?' He smiled kindly and said, 'Not if the person concerned has two sets of cards: that intended for professional use, and that for purely social purposes. I grant that the eccentricity of size could indicate an artist, but it could equally point to a Thespian.' I could not help but ask, somewhat warmly, 'How can you be so sure that he is one rather than the other?' He said, 'Because the stain is caused not by oil paint but by theatrical grease paint.' I demanded to know, 'Have you analysed it?' He chuckled, 'No need, for it is a substance well known to me from its odour and texture. Despite being theatrically involved, Mr Randolph is a man of good education and is at least moderately successful, for the card stock is of good quality and his penned message erudite.'

I dared to enquire, 'Anything else?' Holmes said, with no attempt at effect, 'Not much Doctor, except that he has a number of other appointments to keep and has, possibly, recently resided in the United States. Had he written me a letter I would doubtless know more about him.' I did not bother to enquire how he could deduce these facts from a single written line, because I knew that he would enlighten me.

'The first point, that he has a number of other engagements for this very morning. Were he not pressed for time a man would make an appointment on the hour rather than a quarter to it. My second point, the sojourn, possibly recent, in America: you will notice Watson, the smooth flow of ink in that single written line. This suggests to me that the writer used a recent American invention, the "Reservoir Pen". Need I say more?'

I considered that he did need to enlarge, asking, 'Could he not be an American?' Holmes said, 'Possibly, though from his phrasing I very much doubt it. An American would have stipulated "a quarter *of* ten", he would have used words like "important" or even "desperate" rather than "some urgency". That my dear Watson, is typically British.'

The sound of the doorbell followed by footsteps on the stairs prompted my friend to consult his watch and say, 'Exactly on time Watson, a man of about six feet high and some twelve stone. To the observer, every footstep tells a story.' Having anticipated my question he rose to greet his client.

As Mr Randolph entered I could see that he was indeed only slightly short of six feet in height, well built and neatly dressed in a grey town suit. He was grey haired, with dundreary whiskers, neatly groomed. He had a lively face on which there was an expression of some anxiety.

'Mr Holmes, it's good of you to see me at such short notice. You *are* Sherlock Holmes I presume?' Shaking his hand my friend assured him, 'Yes indeed, and this is my friend and colleague, Dr Watson, before whom you may speak freely. Pray be seated, this chair is tolerably comfortable.' Once seated, Randolph was obviously anxious to get to the purpose of his visit. 'I'm sure you won't know anything about me Mr Holmes, but . . .' Holmes interrupted him, 'On the contrary Mr Randolph, I deduced from your card that you were a busy and punctual man of the theatre, who has spent some time in the United States. Now that we have actually met I can tell that you are in fact a conjurer, and that your American sojourn was in New England.'

Our visitor started, 'Well! Although I used my private card you have obviously seen me perform. I'm flattered that the great detective should spare the time to see a mere conjurer.' Holmes smiled and corrected this false impression. 'I regret to say that I have never seen your performance sir, nor, I regret to say, has your fame preceded you as far as I am concerned.'

Randolph looked more like a puzzled spectator than a conjurer as he gasped, 'Then how . . .'

Holmes related first the deductions made from the card and then said, 'When I shook your hand I noticed a circular depression on your right palm which I consider could only have been caused by many years of regularly holding circular serrated objects, or milled-edged discs in that position. The size is about that of a half crown. Who but a conjurer would regularly "palm" coins?' Randolph was amazed. 'But how could you tell that I had lived in New England?' Holmes explained, 'From your use of the broad "A", among other dialectic tricks.'

'I spent five years in Boston. You are correct all along the line. I've come to the right man, and if anyone can help me you can!' Holmes smiled and said, 'That remains to be seen. Now Mr Randolph, what pray is your predicament?'

We both sat, attentively, as Cyril Randolph told us what was causing his anxiety. 'I am at present engaged to perform twice daily at Maskelyne's Theatre, "The Egyptian Hall," the reputation of which may be known to you even where mine is not?' Holmes nodded, and I could not help asking, 'Does dear old Mr Maskelyne still perform there himself?' Randolph said, 'Why yes, he still spins the odd dinner plate, but leaves most things to young Mr Devant these days.' Holmes, irritated at my interruption waved a restraining hand at me and said to Randolph, 'Pray continue sir.'

'I have a particular trick in my repertoire, a very well known one, in which I borrow a ring from a lady in the audience. This is preferably a ring of some value. This I deliberately smash with a hammer on the pretext of making it fit the barrel of a pistol. I then fire the pistol at a large box. The box is opened to reveal another and this in turn is opened to reveal the last and smallest box. This is opened to expose a nosegay to which a ring is attached by ribbon. Of course, it is the valuable ring, thought to have been smashed.'

He paused, and despite catching Holmes' eye I could not help but interject 'By jove, that's a very old trick, why even I know its secret from reading Professor Hoffmann's "Modern Magic" when I was a student!' Randolph, far from being offended said, 'I agree that it is hackneyed, but the audiences still love it and, despite my other and more original mysteries, they will not allow me to leave it out of my act.'

Holmes, growing impatient with me, said, 'Really Watson, you will do us the service of allowing Mr Randolph to continue uninterrupted by gems from your schoolboy conjuring knowledge! Mr Randolph, pray continue, bearing in mind that I am not about to give you a round of applause.' Both Randolph and I took the hint, resulting in my silence and his effort to reach the point of his trouble. He said to Holmes, 'I am not here to waste your time . . . indeed mine is of value too . . . I want to enlist your help. Two nights ago, at the evening performance I managed to coax the loan of a very valuable diamond ring from a certain Lady Windrush. I performed the trick with it, just as I have described to you, and exactly as I have done a thousand times before . . . only I failed to reproduce her ring. Naturally she is terribly angry and is threatening me with legal proceedings!'

There was a short silence at this point, during which Holmes lit a Turkish cigarette with a vespa. It was he who broke the silence, 'I am not surprised to hear that the lady threatens you with the law. I am unfamiliar with the methods employed by conjurers, and whilst I have no wish to pry into your professional secrets, I fail to see how I can be of help unless you break the code of your craft and explain to me every detail of this trick with the ring.'

Randolph shrugged and said, 'Yes I quite see that Mr Holmes, and as it is a very old trick I see no harm in telling you its method. After all, you have explained something of your methods to me. It happens this way: I step into the audience to borrow the ring. On my way back to the stage I substitute an almost worthless imitation, and palm the genuine ring. I secretly drop the real ring into my assistant's hand as she gives me the pistol. She makes her exit with the real ring as I hammer the worthless one so that I may get it into the barrel of the pistol. Once offstage she attaches the real ring to the nosegay, which she places inside the smallest box. She nests the boxes and brings them onstage. The rest is obvious. However, on the night of question I had the indignity of taking the nosegay from the box to find it quite without any sort of ring attached to it.'

Randolph appeared to have said all that he felt able to

and sat in silence, with a beseeching expression on his face. Holmes worked hard on his cigarette and I knew he was intrigued with the story he had been told. 'From what you have told me, if completely accurate, no one could have handled Lady Windrush's valuable ring save yourself and your assistant. I assume that the lady who assists you can be trusted, otherwise you would have pursued that avenue of explication yourself!'

'Quite so sir, the lady has worked for me for a number of years and has herself a professional reputation to maintain. We are billed as "Cyrano, assisted by Madame Patricia". Her real name is Mabel Cosgrove and I have her assurance that she followed her usual procedure, and you know Mr Holmes, I believe her!'

I risked Holmes' wrath by saying, 'So if the ring really was attached to the nosegay and did not at any stage drop into a crevice in the box . . .' Randolph assured me, 'The boxes are so accurately made that there is no crevice in which anything could lodge. The nest of boxes were carried straight onto the stage after loading. There is no point of possible interception.'

Holmes said, 'There would seem to be no answer short of some sort of necromancy, the existence of which I cannot as a man of science admit to. No further purpose can be gained from prolonging our conversation Mr Randolph.' The Conjurer started, 'You, you mean you will not help me?' Holmes replied, 'On the contrary, I will attend your performance this very evening, to observe for myself that there are no circumstances which could make our bewilderment seem foolish. Be sure to perform the ring trick!'

Randolph was delighted, 'Please Mr Holmes, call at the box office. I will leave a ticket there with your name written upon it.' I coughed insinuatingly. He added, 'In case your colleague should wish to attend, I will leave two tickets.'

After the conjurer had departed Holmes demanded of me, 'Well Watson, what do you make of *that* story?' I said, 'Short of alchemy, there is some aspect of the story that he has left out.' Holmes said, 'Quite so, and had you lost Lady Windrush's valuable diamond ring, would you not have been very concerned indeed?' I answered, 'Randolph seemed worried about it.' Holmes surprised me by saying, '*Seemed*, Watson, that is the word that is the right one, he *seemed* very worried indeed. But the man is an actor, and although he appeared deeply concerned he did not quite ring true.'

Holmes' suspicion surprised me. I said, 'But surely you don't think that Randolph has himself stolen the ring? If he had, would he consult a detective?' My friend said, 'Watson, on the surface you would appear to be right in that. But there are aspects of this that worry me. Why, for instance, has Lady Windrush not consulted the police, rather than simply threatening legal action? If the ring is as valuable as I believe it to be, a woman of such rank and influence would have half of Scotland Yard running around by now. There is more to this situation than we have been told, I think. My dear fellow you are nearer to it than I, so be kind enough to hand me the scrapbook which stands on the shelf between the red one and that file of newsclippings.' I handed my friend the album and he searched through its pages. After perhaps a minute and a half he had discovered what he was looking for: a drawing of a handsome diamond ring, many times its actual size. He stabbed at the picture with his forefinger and his keen eyes travelled down the lines of print which accompanied the drawing. 'Watson, the Windrush ring is infamous! It has already been stolen, ransomed and recovered a number of times. It is worth a quarter of a million pounds, and yet two days after its complete envanishment there is no sort of hue and cry? Indeed this promises to be a more interesting matter than I first supposed.'

As I prepared to depart for the book shop, Holmes threw his cigarette into the fireplace and started to fill an aged clay from the Turkish slipper. He said, 'Watson, on your way back you might drop into the tobacconists and collect the special Scottish-mixture they have promised me for today.'

In the light of the conjurer's extraordinary story, all thoughts concerning my required book had, I confess, left my head. But Holmes forgot nothing. Of course I was intrigued about the true fate of Lady Windrush's ring, and I looked forward to Holmes' possible solution with interest. But even more, I looked forward to our forthcoming visit to 'Maskelyne's', now that I had the perfect excuse to go there.

On my way to the tobacconist's shop (for my visit to the book shop had now become of secondary importance), my eyes lighted upon a splendid pictorial lithograph which had been pasted upon a wall. It advertised 'Maskelyne and Cook's — England's Home of Mystery'. There was a portrait of the celebrated David Devant. Now deep down in every grown man there is a school boy. I remembered a jolly uncle who each Christmas would remove his thumb and produce a shower of comfits from a handkerchief. Later I remembered the discovery of Professor Hoffmann's 'Modern Magic' in a book shop. Of course a boyish desire to become a conjurer had given way to other ambitions, scientific and military. Yet, as I glanced again at that gaily coloured lithograph I realised that the schoolboy in me had never been entirely eliminated. I almost but not quite, felt that tingle of excitement which used to precede a visit to the circus or the pantomime.

When I got back to 221b I found my friend deep in the study of innumerable folders, albums, and scrap-books. He sat, cross-legged upon a rug, smoking a 'hookah' or 'hubble-bubble' which had been a gift from a grateful client, an eastern potentate, who, thanks to Holmes had been able to retain both his head and his throne! A supply of 'special mixture' had been given to Holmes, along with this exotic water-pipe, but to my relief my nose told me that the supply had been exhausted, and that ordinary shag-tobacco had been substituted for it. My friend did not share my pleasure in this substitution, saying, 'You know Watson, that eastern smoking mixture was the strongest I have encountered. I can only hope that some day the Panjandrum will require my services again.'

He indicated the scattering of papers and cuttings with the flexible stem of the pipe. 'You see Watson, I have not been idle. I have searched out everything I own upon the subjects of conjuring, legerdemain and necromancy. During recent years there have been many events involving conjurers which have been considered newsworthy. Many of these "stories", and I use the word advisedly for that is exactly what they are, have one thing in common — they are all much about nothing. Each a pathetic attempt by the subject to gain notoriety. "Conjurer, during trick of death, swallows bullet!" and "The real truth about the Indian Rope Trick"! It is to be hoped that friend Randolph is not aiming to involve us in some form of self advertisement!'

I said, 'Surely Randolph seemed to be intent upon secrecy?' Holmes replied, '*Seemed* Watson, *seemed*. But should he try to involve me in some cheap advertising stunt, he will very much regret it.'

I glanced at one of the cuttings, and asked, 'By the way Holmes, what are your views regarding the Indian rope trick?'

Sherlock Holmes made no reply, but turned upon me a glare, full of venom!

# CHAPTER TWO

# The Egyptian Hall

In order that we should be in good time for the eight o'clock performance at Maskelyne's, at half past seven Billy was sent out into Baker Street to hail a hansom. For once Holmes did not ask if the cab had been the first, second or third to appear. After all, we were not, we thought, engaged in an enterprise which presented any likelihood of danger. Two gentlemen, bound for an enjoyable evening at 'England's Home of Mystery' could raise few eyebrows.

We emerged from Bond Street, into Piccadilly, to rest our eyes upon the familiar sight of the old theatre, Maskelyne's painted facade partly obscuring two giant, undraped statues which stood as ever, one above each entrance corner. The partial obscurity was for reasons of publicity rather than any sort of prudery. The advertising board promised, 'ANIMATED PHOTOGRAPHS . . . THE FINEST IN LONDON!' On viewing this signboard, Holmes remarked, 'I am a little surprised that such a showman should exhibit the cinematograph, which if I am not mistaken, within a few short years, months even, will be taken for granted.' I agreed, but was secretly pleased that we should see this marvel of science. I had seen it once before, from the Empire promenade, but it had been a poor, flickering demonstration sandwiched between the turns of Little Tich and Marie Lloyd: besides which, my attention had been distracted by other matters.

The theatre's facade was deceptive, and from its presentation one could be forgiven for expecting some vast auditorium rather than the delightful little theatre with its intimate drawing room atmosphere. An air of mystery was heightened by an overture being played by an orchestra of 'invisible musicians'. The instruments hung above a gallery and the music appeared to emerge from them, yet no hands were seen plucking their strings nor mouths blowing at their mouthpieces.

As for the performance itself, why it was capital. From the elderly J.N. Maskelyne spinning his dinner plates, the sedate and charismatic David Devant conjuring eggs from a hat and bringing the portrait of a young woman to life, to the dramatic magical sketch presided over by young Nevil Maskelyne. It all brought back such happy memories of a dozen other such evenings, so many years before. I remembered those quaintly phrased claims in the printed programme, 'All natural laws cast aside . . . The fakirs of the east robbed of their secrets and the scientists of Europe stripped of their cunning'. Ah, happy days. Now as one of those 'scientists of Europe' I felt that I knew how most of these wonders were accomplished. I turned to Holmes once or twice to give him the benefit of my theories but received no reply. Then, during a short interval between two items, he turned to me and said, sternly, 'Watson, the sophisticated mind is the easiest to deceive through theatrical necromancy. Only children and those adults of limited intellect are able to resist the magician's misdirection of the senses. I for one have no intention whatever of trying to solve these particular mysteries. More, I would greatly appreciate it if you would cease to give me the benefit of your lack of imagination. The appearance upon the stage of friend Randolph will be your cue to become alert.'

It was fortunate perhaps that the presentation which followed was not of a deceptive nature. Watching two jugglers openly display their sheer skill and dexterity enabled my feelings to calm. After all, there is nothing more frustrating than to have a secret and be unable to share it with a friend!

I glanced at my programme to learn that the next item would also be non-controversial, as far as Holmes and I were concerned. 'Stella, the Stenographic Marvel' would be something mechanical which would create wonderment without attempt at deception.

The exhibition of 'automata' had long been a regular occurance at the Egyptian Hall. In fact I could remember seeing old J.N. Maskelyne himself presenting the most famous of these, 'Psycho': a small oriental figure capable of writing the answers to questions upon a slate. Now his son, Nevil, presented the latest in the Maskelyne tradition of mechanical wonders. 'Stella', a small and beautifully modelled female figure sat behind a desk of proportionate size. She was appropriately dressed to represent a lady-typewriter operator and upon the desk stood the typewriting machine itself. Young Maskelyne fed a piece of paper into it, and in the usual manner bade 'Stella' to 'Take a letter'. He dictated fairly slowly as the tiny hands pounded upon the keys. Eventually, when he had finished dictating he moved the paper from the machine and read it aloud to the audience. It was of course the same message which we had heard him dictate. . .

Maskelyne's Theatre
London
March 21st, 1898

To our esteemed patrons.

Dear Friends,

We are happy to see you again, and we hope you will like this new programme of brand new mysteries.

Many of you will remember 'Psycho', and now we are proud to introduce 'Stella', who represents the spirit of the new age in which members of the fair sex are beginning to take their place in commerce. Their delicacy of touch makes them particularly well adapted for the operation of the new typewriting machines, one of the earliest of which was developed and built by my father, J.N. Maskelyne. Now he has built a young lady to operate it!

Yours sincerely,
Nevil Maskelyne

Many in the audience at this point believed that young Maskelyne was trying to hoodwink them by simply repeating what he had already dictated, and pretending to read it off a blank sheet of paper. I confess that had I not seen 'Psycho' I might have suspected as much myself. But Maskelyne disproved such deceit by passing the letter to a cleric in the front row, who verified the letter and passed it to a doubter who asked to see it. Further doubts were dispelled when young Nevil allowed persons in the audience to dictate short letters to the automata, which it typed and Maskelyne duly passed to them to read aloud.

Finally the magician opened up the front of the desk, exposing the clockwork mechanism. I applauded as loudly as anyone, though I felt that the figure, despite its comely appearance, had not the dignity or versatility, nay even the mystery which had surrounded 'Psycho'.

Holmes leaned forward in his seat and whispered to me, 'I would like a closer view of the mechanism.' I said nothing, mechanics not being my strong point.

During the interlude we strolled in the vestibule and had an opportunity to study the audience. They were, I decided, unlike any other London theatre audience. Although the programme had some hint of the vaudeville about it, there were never at Maskelyne's any of those acts that might be termed vulgar. Therefore the patrons were not those of the music hall. As I looked around me I saw dukes, dustmen, titled ladies and retired clerics. The nearest similarity would be found in the audience attracted by the D'oyly Carte Opera Company. There were some children, but I noticed that each child had a number of adults in tow, not just parents but uncles, aunties and friends, anxious not to miss the fun.

In Palm Court we sipped our Turkish coffee and ruminated upon what we had seen. Holmes remarked sagely, 'I find the conjurers far more interesting than their deceptions!'

That my friend was serious in his claim to be deceived by simple showmans' tricks, I doubted. But with his mood of the moment I dared say no more on the subject. The interval over, we enjoyed the antics of a sad-faced clown who cavorted merrily enough, imitating various musical instruments. Then we were intrigued by a transatlantic gentleman billed as 'Shifty Jack'. He picked the pockets of a number of gentlemen in the audience, amazing them with the return of each wallet, watch and cigar case. Holmes was very interested in this demonstration.

At long last there entered upon the scene our client, Mr Cyril Randolph, or 'Cyrano' as the programme named him. He looked very different in his tails; he seemed taller, and his grey dundrearys had been limned with black. He made an 'entrance' with style and grace, handing his opera hat and gloves to his lady assistant. Covering the ends of a small tube with paper, he converted it into a tambourine which he then burst, producing from it a score of gaily coloured squares of silk and cambric. The music ceased and he addressed the audience with fake foreign tones, presumably intended to be a French accent.

'Ladies and Gentlemen, I am not an Englishman so I 'ope you can understand my words. I will please my best to "do" you, no? I am not a poor man, yet I wish to borrow . . . from one of you . . . a ring . . . with the sparkley stones!' Within half a minute he had coaxed a seemingly valuable diamond ring from a prosperous looking gentleman in the stalls.

'Please take a good look at your ring Sir, so that you will recognise it if you ever . . . excuse me, *when* you see it again!' The conjurer coughed in mock embarrassment at his own deliberate 'slip of the tongue'.

We watched keenly as he returned to the stage, but neither Holmes nor I, in later discussion, could name the exact moment when the substitution was made. Certainly from the theatre stalls it would have been impossible to know that the ring he held in the limelight was not that which we had just seen him borrow. He had told us that he invariably smashed the ring, and, although forewarned and aware of the substitution, such was the drama of his presentation that we all but gasped as he smote it with a hammer in order that it would fit the barrel of his gun. The audience gasped too, and then resorted to laughter which seemed to be the only sensible reaction. He cocked an expressive eyebrow, saying, 'Why do you laugh . . . you wouldn't if it were yours . . . The kind gentleman who lent me the ring . . . *he* is not laughing!'

'Madame Patricia', a handsome, flaxen-haired young

woman of buxom build, made an exit carrying a tray bearing the properties from his handkerchief trick off-stage. As she departed Holmes whispered, 'You see, he has dropped the genuine ring onto the tray.' I replied, 'We hardly need your "methods" to know that!' He admonished, 'Come Watson, we have both been told how the trick is done, so are you not being wise after the event?'

The conjurer finished his whimsey of stuffing the now ruined ring into the revolver barrel. After a few more pleasantries he called, 'Madame Patricia . . . my magic box if you please!' The pianist played furiously as the lady re-entered bearing a mahogany box on a tray. Cyrano raised his pistol and fired. The result was much red fire and smoke, but very little by way of explosion. The music quietened as he said, 'Patricia, pray open the box and take from it that which you find inside.' She opened the box and withdrew from it another box of only very slightly smaller proportions. This in turn revealed a smaller box, inside which there proved to be a nosegay or posey, to which was attached a ring.

I remarked to Holmes, 'She must work fast to attach that ring to the flower and nest the boxes.' Holmes said, 'She gains much more time than one would think, with the audience laughing at Cyrano's banter. A task oft repeated becomes easier and less time consuming. In any case, she has a full two minutes to do what she has to.' Holmes had been timing each phase of the experiment, but this had not prevented his shrewd observance of every move. He still watched keenly as the conjurer returned the ring to the affluent one, with the gift of a flower for his buttonhole. We were about to discuss that which we had seen when our attention was gained by Cyrano in the presentation of what would prove to be his final illusion. I had never seen anything like it until that night, and have never seen its like since. Therefore, I feel it is noteworthy enough for me to describe fully.

Madame Patricia entered, carrying a very small leather bag: rather like a slightly smaller version of the bag in which I carry my medical equipment. She handed this to Cyrano with due solemnity. He opened the bag with equal propriety and as she made her exit, he took from the bag a small square box, no more than a foot high. This he placed upon a small undraped table and, walking to the foot-lights, he signalled to the pianist to stop playing. He said, 'Ladies and Gentlemen, inside that box is my wife!' There was much laughter at the thought of the possibility of a grown woman being inside such a small compass. He frowned in mock severity at the laughter of the audience. 'You do not believe me? Very well then, watch closely and you will see something which you will remember for the rest of your lives. Watch!'

The pianist recommenced playing, feverishly in fact, as the small box suddenly and quite unaccountably increased in size. After a few more seconds the box began a second stage in its enlargement, until it was the size of a large packing case.

What we had thus far seen was startling indeed. But this was as nothing compared with what we were still to witness. Cyrano lifted the large box that he had created, revealing a very substantial lady! It was indeed the very same Madame Patricia who had brought the box on stage in its original state, in the now seemingly inadequate leather bag. She stood there on the little table, a large lady looking even larger than usual in a Merry-Widow hat and leg-of-mutton sleeves.

'Well Doctor,' Holmes snapped at me, as loudly as was possible short of disturbing the audience, 'will you kindly explain to me the modus operandi of this enigma? I feel sure that with the advantage of having read Professor Hoffmann's "Modern Magic" you must know the secret?' But the explanation of this puzzle had (and I was forced to confess it) even eluded myself.

As for the audience, they were truly amazed, even slightly alarmed at what they had seen. They had assembled to be bamboozled by conjurers, but expected what they might see to have at least a possibility of explanation. Here however, was what appeared to be real magic, and this feeling somewhat delayed their show of appreciation.

Alas, for Cyrano, an interruption prevented that well merited round of applause from even starting. For there arose from a seat in the stalls a small, thick-set man, with a mane of wild hair and a full beard who bellowed a protest in a distinctly foreign accent:

'Stop, do not give him your claps pliz . . . he is a thief! He has stolen my invention, my wonderful expanding cube . . . I have worked on it for years and I am still rehearsalling with it . . . yet even now he has it, this thief! But I, Buatier De Kolta, I will kill him!'

Holmes muttered, 'An amazingly dramatic interruption Watson. Hear his voice as it shakes with passion. He is either a Hungarian with Parisian domicile or a Frenchman who has lived in Hungary, for his accent carries both elements.' Two burly theatre attendants bore down upon the little man and assisted him in leaving the building. His cries of 'That thief, I will kill him' could still be faintly heard after the access doors had slammed shut behind him.

Cyrano had wisely retired from the stage and the curtain was down by the time the demented little man had been removed from the scene. With great enterprise the management chose this moment to drop a screen of the type used by magic-lantern showmen, from the wings of the theatre.

Despite this distraction the 'Animated Photographs' glued us to our seats and soon caused the audience to forget all about the angry little foreigner and his threats to kill Cyrano. They were not only amazed but truly alarmed as the Brighton to London express train rushed toward them. They twitched and flinched, but were soon beguiled by a moving depictation of Queen Victoria's Jubilee. Although the pictures jumped and flickered it was possible to make out the faces and figures of the great personalities involved. The sight of the German Kaiser was greeted by cries of 'Willy. . . There's old Willy!' and the Prince of Wales was 'Good old Ted!' As for the Queen in her carriage it was a case of 'God Save the Queen!'

'Celebrities in the Park', so said the lettering on the sheet, followed by a number of unrelated 'scenes', (as they were called in the theatre) of people, animals and events. The only thread of connection was that all were evidently photographed (or 'cinephotographed') in a park. There were nursemaids flirting with soldiers, famous people with their dogs, and policemen on bicycles. This theme gave way to what purported to be an actual filming of the Heavyweight Fight between Guardsman Gray and Charles McDougal, which we well knew had taken place only a week or two earlier.

'Upon my word!' Holmes could not contain himself, as he explained to me 'sotto voice' that he had attended that particular pugilistic contest, and could state quite definitely that neither of the fighters depicted were genuine. 'Actors have recreated the contest . . . blow by blow. I'll wager Maskelyne doesn't know that he is presenting a fake!'

Having only seen a newspaper artist's impression of either man, most of the audience were willing to accept the fight as genuine. After all, the right contestant won!

The next episode to gain our attention (although the flickering of the images upon the sheet had by now tired our eyes), was titled 'Adventures with Sherlock Holmes'. Two actors, the one tall and slim, wearing an Inverness cape and deerstalker, the other, shorter and inclined to corpulance, were evidently intended to represent ourselves. The makers of this episode had obviously been influenced by my account of the adventure of 'The Speckled Band' in the Strand, for the tall actor thrashed at a very unrealistic snake descending a bell rope. The episode was mercifully short. It prompted Holmes to turn to me and say, 'See what you have done Watson . . . your literary vanity has made us both into figures of fun!'

There followed a comedy 'film' (as I have since heard such episodes called) in which a thief attempted to creep up upon an old lady asleep in a chair outside her cottage. His intention was to steal her canary from its cage. The laughter which this merry scene occasioned was continued by the antics of a knockabout music hall pair. There was of course no speech or other sound as there would have been if they performed in a theatre, but an energetic pianist and the novelty of it compensated for this.

Then, quite suddenly and right in the middle of 'A View from Putney Bridge of the Oxford and Cambridge University boat race', David Devant walked out in front of the screen and signalled the pianist to cease his efforts. It took a little longer for the projectionist to cease, the momentary continuation of images giving a strange and eerie effect to Devant's usually handsome features. At last the screen went blank and the auditorium lights were raised. In a loud, clear, but unhurried voice, Devant asked, 'Ladies and Gentlemen, is there a doctor in the house?'

# CHAPTER THREE

# The Dressing Room of Death

As David Devant made his dramatic appeal, 'Is there a doctor in the house?' I found myself raising a hand and briskly mounting the tiny flight of steps which bridged the stage and auditorium. He greeted me with an urgent warmth, saying quietly, 'There's been a serious accident.' Then in a louder voice he spoke to the audience, 'Ladies and Gentlemen, due to unforeseen circumstances tonight's performance is now concluded. We hope to see you all again . . .' His words tailed off, drowned by the shrewd pianist who had commenced a spirited rendition of 'God Save the Queen'. As the patrons filed out, muttering 'What's up?' and 'Wonder who's hurt?', Devant explained to me, 'It's Cyrano, he's dead . . . or, at least that is the view of a non medical man.' I hastily introduced my friend, and we hurried through the backstage area as Devant steered us toward the dressing room where Cyrano was lying.

The door of Cyrano's dressing room was ajar, and as we

stepped inside one glance at his inert form told me that Devant was right. I could see from his expression and protruding tongue that he was very dead indeed. Still in his evening clothes and theatrical make-up, he lay, gazing glassily up at us.

I dropped swiftly to my knees and tried to find some sign of life. Finding no pulse I put an ear to his chest but detected no heart-beat (I had no stethoscope having worn my opera-hat to the theatre). Finally I resorted to the old trick of holding a hand mirror to his mouth, but it produced no reassuring sign. I looked at the discolourations at his throat and felt the back of his head. I declared, 'Life is quite extinct. In my opinion the cause of death is strangulation, and possibly a broken neck, though a police surgeon will need to establish this exactly. This man has died in a brutal attack by someone with enormous strength, would you not agree Holmes?'

My friend, ever practical, yet mindful of the fact that I was the expert first called upon, had thus far stood back. Now he began to assume command. 'The bruises on the throat indicate an attack by a man with very large hands and as you say Doctor, enormous strength. After all, Cyrano, or rather Mr Randolph was a strongly built man of considerable physique. Mr Devant, I suggest that you send a member of your staff to summon the police.' Devant nodded and left us in the room with the body. As soon as he was out of earshot Holmes added, 'Meanwhile I must learn what I can before the police trample over what little evidence there may be.'

The room was fairly typical of its kind, with a dressing table before a wide wall mirror. Holmes gave his attention first to the only egress from the room apart from the door. This proved to be a partly raised sash window of extremely narrow dimensions. I asked, 'Do you think the killer made his escape through that window Holmes?' He looked a little doubtful saying, 'Whilst we cannot entirely rule out the possibility Watson, it would have to have been a very wiry man indeed. I might manage it myself, despite my height, with a struggle, but a well built fellow such as yourself would find it impossible. Have we not established that the crime would have involved a man of great strength?'

Holmes opened a closet, to find only the conjurer's street clothes and greatcoat hanging. The rest of the room was occupied by the impedimenta of illusion: silk scarves, tripod-tables and the mahogany boxes for the famous ring trick. On the bench lay scattered sticks of grease-paint, boxes of powder, towels that had been used to clean off make-up, and a bottle of liquid-paraffin which would have assisted this process. Also there lay there a fancy wooden box, to which Holmes gave his attention. 'A make-up box?' I enquired. He shook his head. 'No Watson, it is a puzzle-box, of oriental design. I have come across these before. The owner uses them to contain his valuables and only he knows how to open it. There is no key involved.' I asked, 'Then how . . .' But Holmes had anticipated this question and was demonstrating how the lid closure could be released by pressure upon a portion of the base, followed by pushing a portion of the lid. It was ingenius though not profound. As the lid was opened it was revealed that the box was empty save for a small length of thin red ribbon, about six inches long. I said, 'A toy no doubt, of the kind indulged in by a man who admires the ingenius. Possibly Randolph has been to China?' Holmes said, 'It is possible Watson, but he bought this box in this country I imagine. You will observe the words "Made in

China" stamped upon the bottom. In China the words would have been in one of the dialects of that huge country.'

Holmes worked quickly, as if his ear had already detected the distant tread of the heavy booted constabulary. Had the circumstances been less grave I would have been forced to smile at the way he urgently peered into this and opened that, rather with the air of one woman secretly inspecting the kitchen of another. The window sill and the floor in the general area of that aperture held his attention for quite a while. He said, 'There are footprints, or, to be more exact, footmarks. But they are extremely indistinct and may not even be recent. Yet assuming that the dressing rooms receive some sort of daily cleaning, the most lax of domestics could hardly have failed to notice these wood shavings.'

He collected up some scraps of what looked to me like pencil sharpenings. Taking a used envelope from his inside pocket he deposited them within. When I enquired if they were indeed hewn from a pencil he said, 'No, although they are cedar they have been produced not with a knife but rather with a small spokeshave. It may be that a carpenter has recently climbed out of this window.'

When the police made their appearance, in the shape of a uniformed constable and two plain clothes men I was not a little surprised to find that one of those in mufti was our old colleague, Inspector Lestrade.

'Mr Holmes, Doctor . . . as soon as I heard that you were involved I made it my business to take charge of this affair.' He glanced at the body, not entirely unaffected. 'Grisly business eh? I'm sure that you have some of the answers by now, for it has taken us an annoyingly long time to get here from the Yard.' Holmes said, politely, 'I could wish, Inspector, for our reunion to have been under happier circumstances. The deceased man is, or was, Mr Cyril Randolph, a conjurer, known professionally as "Cyrano". He was a client of mine. Doctor Watson and I were here at his invitation, to see his performance. The very last thing we expected to round off a pleasant evening was the sight of his dead body!'

Lestrade bent down and made a perfunctory examination of the body, soon enquiring of me, 'Strangulation Doctor?' I nodded, adding, 'And a fractured neck I fancy, but your own man can verify that.' He said, 'Quite so, Doctor Simpsom will be here directly.'

Between us, Holmes and I told Lestrade the whole story of Cyril Randolph, the reason for his visit to Baker Street, and the events of the evening which had culminated in the tragedy. Lestrade made notes as we spoke, and seemed more than a little interested in our account of the bearded foreigner who had interrupted the performance. He asked, 'You say he actually threatened to kill this Randolph, making the threat in front of hundreds of people, and all over a conjuring trick?' I said, 'Had you seen the illusion Inspector, you would realise that it was far from a run of the mill deception.' He grunted, and we continued, Holmes remarking, 'I believe the threat to have been uttered in the heat of temper, and not really to be taken literally. Why Inspector if you took seriously every wife's threat to kill her husband you would have your work cut out'. Lestrade said, 'Nevertheless, if their husbands turned up dead soon after they had said it, I would count them as suspects!'

With the arrival of the police surgeon we left the dressing room and entered another, larger apartment which Devant had made available to Lestrade. Those members of the cast of Maskelyne's show who had not already left the theatre at the time of the tragedy were present, as were some members of the theatre staff. The constable and the plain clothes sergeant had arranged this.

Lestrade looked around the room and seemingly addressed everyone present, enquiring, 'Who found the body?'

Without rising from her chair the dead conjurer's lady assistant spoke, 'I did Inspector. I occupy the dressing room used by several other ladies of the company. I went to Mr Cyril's room to ask him at what o'clock he would require me on the morrow, only to find him lying there. I am not a nervous person, but I admit that I screamed, and am trembling still from the sight of poor Cyril's face, so horribly distorted!'

Lestrade, considerate to her in his manner, asked a few pertinent questions. 'The window was open Miss?'

'Yes, just a little, at the bottom.'

'And you disturbed nothing?'

'Why, no, there was little point, for I could see from his appearance that he was dead. I backed out of the room almost at once, and then I think I screamed.'

'Who responded first when you raised the alarm?'

She thought carefully before she replied, then said, 'There were several persons who arrived almost at once. It is hard to say who reached me first, for I was in a dazed state. I believe the first to try and calm me was Jack, the pickpocket, I know him by no other name. There were the two clowns and Miss Glenrose, who shares my dressing room. She is the lady in the portrait which comes to life.'

Lestrade, I noticed, made no notes, but his sergeant was busily writing down everything which was said. Holmes and I were careful not to interrupt these official enquiries, but I could see that my friend was devouring every word spoken. The inspector confirmed Miss Patricia's statement by questioning the people that she had named. As he did so, Holmes took the opportunity to use me as a sounding board for his own thoughts.

'Consider that which we know Watson. Cyrano was very much alive and in plain view of several hundred people but ten minutes before the discovery of his body. We can eliminate the two ladies involved, Miss Patricia and Miss Glenrose, because the fatal action called for enormous strength on the part of the murderer. The pickpocket and the clowns do not appear to be robust enough either, although one cannot rule them out completely. It would take someone of Devant's build for example to commit such an act.' I gasped, 'Surely you don't think . . .' But Holmes stopped me by saying, 'No Watson, I think that unlikely, though he may well have been the last to see Cyrano alive.' I enquired, 'What makes you think so?' The detective smiled enigmatically and said, 'Watson, Devant is the manager of the whole enterprise. Cyrano's act was interrupted and the moving pictures had to be quickly brought into play. I feel sure that Devant must have been responsible for the programme change, and may even have spoken to Cyrano in the theatre wings, aye and even in the ill-fated dressing room itself.'

From the corner of my eye I could see Lestrade in quiet but animated converse with Devant. Holmes, seemingly unobservent of this was, I knew, fully aware of the conversation. He lit a cigarette, obviously craving stronger tobacco, but unable to sooth his craving. As he studied the burning tip of the Egyptian cigarette, Lestrade addressed him.

'Mr Holmes, I have discovered that Mr Devant was the last person present who saw Cyrano alive, and spoke with him.' Holmes nodded wisely, and his right eyelid dropped a fraction of an inch, for my benefit. 'Indeed, Inspector?' 'Yes sir, and what is more, he is the only one here big and strong enough to have committed the crime!'

Holmes mused, 'So you seriously consider that the world celebrated and respected illusionist, junior partner of the even more celebrated Maskelyne and Cooke, would throw away a great career in such an irresponsible manner? Not impossible I'll grant you, but knowing you as I do Inspector, I feel sure that you have established an extremely strong motive for the crime.'

I felt a pang of sympathy for Lestrade, as he opened and closed his mouth two or three times before saying, 'Oh I don't actually suspect him Mr Holmes, although everyone must be considered. No, it's this foreign fellow that I believe must be our man!'

Holmes stubbed out the cigarette with some irritation and said, 'You mean Buatier De Kolta, the man who interrupted the performance just a mere ten minutes before the crime was committed?'

The inspector clicked his fingers to summon his sergeant, and bade him write the name 'Buatier De Kolta' in his book. I was amazed that Holmes could remember the name, heard but once under such conditions, which I could not have recalled myself. Lestrade, confident again, started to express his theories. 'This, er - De Kolta, evidently stood up in the audience and loudly stated that he would kill Cyrano, and from what I have learned he is a very strongly built man, capable of the crime!'

The Baker Street freelance looked keenly at the official arm of the finest detective force in the world and said, 'If De Kolta committed this crime, and I do not at this stage suggest that it is impossible, he must have entered the dressing room by its door.'

Lestrade fell into the trap. 'The window was open!'

'Quite, but we have established that only a man of wiry build could have entered by it. De Kolta was escorted from the premises, only minutes before the event. If he is guilty of the murder he must have re-entered the building by other means. But then I have no doubt that you have already interrogated the stage door keeper and all of the front of house staff.' Holmes spoke the words not as a question, which might have embarrassed the Scotland Yard man. As it was, Inspector Lestrade was able to save his face by nodding curtly, saying, 'Excuse me, I must pursue my enquiries . . .'

With the inspector off the scene, Holmes wasted no time in pursuing a few enquiries of his own. The first person he made towards was David Devant.

Mr Devant invited Holmes and I to join him in his 'lair' (as he called it) which proved to be a spacious apartment on an upper floor of the Egyptian Hall. He was circumspect enough to suggest that the permission of Inspector Lestrade should be sought before he left the green room. However, Holmes assured him that this would hardly be necessary. This assurance was borne out when we passed Lestrade in the corridor, where he was interviewing the elderly stage door keeper. He merely nodded curtly as we passed, without any questions as to Devant's intended movements.

Devant's lair was a strange mixture of the administrative and the theatrical, with its framed posters and huge roll-top desk. There were several comfortable-looking chairs, and he bade us take advantage of two of these, which we did, Devant himself preferring to perch upon a high stool, of the kind used by clerks and secretaries. He told us a good deal about himself, and how he had been taken on by Maskelyne just a few years earlier.

'I was a nomad Mr Holmes, touring the music halls, and sometimes broadening my activities. Why once I even managed a troupe of midgets. But I settled here, first as a performer, but later able to take some of the responsibilities from Mr Maskelyne's shoulders. Now I am manager of the Egyptian Hall, and a junior partner to Maskelyne and Cooke. The Guv'nor trusts me completely, a trust, I might add, I would never abuse. The only real difference we have ever had concerned the moving pictures. When I saw Trewey's demonstration at the polytechnic I knew we had to have them. The old man wouldn't buy a projector, so I purchased one myself, and he could hardly refuse its use. Through its introduction he has seen a considerable improvement at the box-office.'

He offered us refreshment, bringing spirit and gasogyne bottles from a well stocked cupboard. I noticed that he poured more than a generous measure of spirit into his own glass. Though he showed no other signs of nervousness, I noted a slight tremor of his right hand.

I had seen only the brief appearance of Mr Maskelyne, and no sign of him since. I asked, 'Does Mr Maskelyne also have an office in the building?' 'Oh yes, right at the top, like an eyrie. It's more of a workshop really. You know he is a mechanical genius. Apart from theatrical automata he has innovated many commercial items. He built one of the first practical typewriting machines, and invented the penny in the slot contrivance that is used in most public lavatories.'

Holmes asked, 'Has he been informed of the tragedy?' Devant nodded. 'Oh yes, his son Nevil has surely told him. But the inspector thought it unnecessary to question him. After all, he was up in his attic at the time of the murder.'

Holmes, irritated by his long abstinence from strong tobacco asked, 'Have you by chance some of that Rhodesian shag that you smoke, and a spare pipe?' the conjurer shot a sharp glance at the detective, and then relaxed into a smile of comprehension. As he brought a pipe and pouch from a desk drawer he said, 'I hadn't realised that its odour lingered so, I am so used to it.' Holmes chuckled, mellowed by the thought that he would soon be consuming strong shag again. 'I too am used to it, but my reaction to its scent is sharpened by long deprivation.'

As the strong smoke began to fill the room, Devant leaned earnestly forward and asked, 'Mr Holmes, how may I help you? For I realise that although you are conducting enquiries in this grim business, it could not have been that which brought you here. Moreover, I would judge that a musical recital would be more your idea of entertainment than an exhibition of necromancy! Did some prediction of tragedy bring you here?'

Holmes chuckled through the comforting fumes of Rhodesian shag and said, 'Cyrano was a client of mine Mr Devant. We came here at his invitation. But despite the fact that he has expired, I cannot at this present moment divulge his confidence.'

Devant responded, 'You are so right to respect his confidence.'

Holmes changed the subject. 'Tell me, are you able to actually make your own films, as well as simply showing those which already exist?' Devant showed some surprise at this enquiry, but also seemed happy enough to answer it in an open manner. 'Why yes, I have a special camera with which I am able to do so. I myself made the film of Queen Victoria's Jubilee, which you saw this evening.'

A knock on the door interrupted what might have proved to be a most interesting conversation. It was Lestrade, with the news that he had concluded his investigations for the time being.

'I'm going back to the Yard. Can I offer you a lift gentlemen?'

43

I nodded, but Holmes cancelled my nod by shaking his head and saying, 'It is kind of you Inspector, but it is a pleasant evening. I think a walk back to Baker Street might help my chain of thought.'

Lestrade left us, his only other comment being to the effect that on the morrow he would question Buatier De Kolta. 'I have not the evidence to arrest him, but I certainly want a few words with that gentleman!'

We said our goodbyes to Devant, who assured Holmes that he would be given the freedom of the Egyptian Hall at any time.

We strolled at a steady pace that would have been a perfect example to a newly recruited police constable, had Holmes' angular frame not leaned forward, as it tended to when he was deep in thought. We gained Oxford Street by way of New Bond Street, and eventually turned into Baker Street itself for the final three quarter miles of our walk.

Several times we passed rowdy mobs of troublemakers, strayed from their native East End. Holmes appeared not to notice them and possibly did not. Anyway I was grateful that he and I did not present the appearance of easy victims. I fancied my stout malacca would have set them to flight had the situation arisen. I was comforted also by the fact that Holmes was the finest boxer, for his weight, in the whole of England.

Several times I was tempted to hail a hansom, but dared not lest I disturb my friend's reverie.

Then, almost within sight of home he spoke. 'Watson, we went to the Egyptian Hall to investigate a robbery, and stayed to enquire into a murder most foul. On the surface the two things would appear to be unconnected yet my mind tells me that a connection there must be!'

As we stood upon the doorstep of 221b I was weary, for

the hour was late. Yet from the light of the street lamp I could detect the animation in my friend's face, aye and the sparkle in his eyes.

# CHAPTER FOUR

# A Visit Returned

**M**r Sherlock Holmes' breakfast habits and manner-
isms I have well documented in the past but, on the
morning following our visit to the Egyptian Hall, I
entered the living room to find that there had been no
arrangements for breakfast whatever. Holmes, fully
dressed in a town suit, sat at the unlaid table, his letters,
newspapers and a telegram before him.

'Watson! Your tardiness has at last caught up with you.
Breakfast was over long ago!'

In panic I consulted my turnip, only to find that my
bedroom clock had not been inaccurate. Then I caught the
twinkle in my friend's eye.

'No Watson, it is not long past your usual time for
making your entrance. I have found it necessary to postpone, or even eliminate breakfast entirely.' I found all this
a little breathtaking, for the cancellation of breakfast at
221b Baker Street must surely, I felt, indicate some event
of great import. In trying to imagine what the event could
be a sudden stab of sad possibility crossed my mind.

'Holmes . . . Her Gracious Majesty. . . .' He interrupted, 'Well and hearty to the best of my knowledge Watson.' I glanced at the newspapers and Holmes caught the direction of my glance. 'Nothing in the morning papers that would make it necessary for us to miss breakfast.'

Then I looked at the telegram upon his plate, half revealing an expensive looking envelope upon which I could see half of a family crest. He still followed my gaze and said, 'Right at last Watson, for the telegram announces the impending visit of Mr David Devant. He will be with us within a quarter of an hour.'

I said, 'Which means that he has something to tell you which he did not remember, or wish to tell you last night. However, he wishes to tell you now, yet does not wish to take Lestrade into his confidence.'

Holmes applauded me.

'Excellent Watson, I am of the same mind, and we can confirm or deny our predictions within a few minutes. Meanwhile, you may just have time to cast your eye over this item in "The Courier".'

He passed me the newspaper, neatly folded, so that the item which he wished me to read was isolated. As he handed it to me I was given a tantalising glimpse of that crested envelope. But he swiftly transferred that elegant seeming missive to his inside pocket. I did not ask him about the letter, instead giving my attention to the newspaper piece.

## TERRIBLE TRAGEDY AT
## MASKELYNE'S THEATRE

The Egyptian Hall, 'England's Home of Mystery', was the scene last night of a tragic mystery to rival any dramatic necromancy of Mr J.N. Maskelyne. Cyril Randolph, known professionally as 'Cyrano', was found brutally murdered in his dressing room only minutes after giving a performance which had been interrupted by death threats. The man who uttered those threats, the eminent French illusionist, Buatier De Kolta, far from being in custody, is to replace the late Mr Randolph in the Egyptian Hall programme!

Holmes had neatly underlined the last paragraph with a red pencil.

I laid the paper back on the table. 'Why Holmes, the decision to include De Kolta in the programme must have been very quickly made, and is, if I might say so, in the worst possible taste.'

Holmes chuckled, 'Come Watson, we are dealing here with showmen.'

I grunted, 'Devant must have known about this before we left the Egyptian Hall last night, for the news to appear in this morning's paper.' He shook his head, 'I doubt it, indeed I fancy we should have cast our better feelings aside and visited the old gentleman in the attic.'

'Maskelyne . . . you think this is his doing? Yet Devant told us of his unenterprising attitude toward the moving pictures.' Holmes replied, 'Yes, but that was an invention which, strangely I'll grant, had failed to capture his imagination. He is an old showman with a great sense of the dramatic. But as far as Devant is concerned, there is a certain other matter in which I would have preferred him to confide in me.'

Before I could rejoin, substantial footsteps hailed the arrival of David Devant. As he entered, the conjurer looked very different from the man in the faultless tails the night before. His country tweed suit, hat, and ashplant made him look like a country squire. We seated him almost as comfortably as he had seated us in his lair. He declined tobacco from the slipper but accepted a cigar from the coalscuttle.

'Mr Holmes, Doctor Watson, it is good of you to see me at such an hour, but I had to see you and my day is so filled. My first business appointments are at ten, followed by rehearsals at eleven. Then I have to prepare the theatre for the reception of the public, who will start to arrive for the matinee at two-thirty. Then I have that performance and another in the evening. I will be home at midnight with any luck.'

I enquired, 'At what hour do you rise sir?'

He replied, 'At six, and I ride on Hampstead Heath between seven and eight. So you see I am usually very direct, for my crowded life makes this necessary. But I have been less than direct with you Mr Holmes and I am here to put that right.'

Holmes said, 'Little explanation is required Mr Devant. The circumstances of the mislaid diamond ring, the mechanics of the performance and other circumstances make its loss all but impossible. I do not of course suggest that Randolph intended to steal it. If he had he would hardly have engaged a detective to find it. No, he engaged me because he was sure that I would *not* find it. After all, he had it safe himself, or so he thought. As for the titled lady, he established just how long it would be before she enlisted the law. He planned to "find" the ring again, publicly, under bizarre circumstances at a performance. The whole thing then was what you showmen would term a "publicity device" and would be well documented in the newspapers. But he could not have attempted the scheme I feel without your own co-operation.'

I was genuinely surprised. Devant also looked amazed, but what amazed him was that Holmes had told him what he had called to say. He said, 'You have deduced everything correctly. It was a daring idea, which was what appealed to me when Cyrano came to me with it. Yes, it was daring, but not dangerous until now.'

Holmes said 'You mean now that the diamond ring really has disappeared?'

Devant nodded glumly and Holmes continued, 'I imagine he kept it in the Chinese puzzle box in his dressing room. I shook the box last evening, and there was no reassuring rattle.'

I could not help but interrupt, 'Could we now have a motive for the murder . . . The ring I mean?'

Holmes said, 'Possibly. Certainly whoever took the ring knew the secret of the box. Otherwise it would have been broken open or it would be missing.'

Devant was obviously astonished that Holmes had taken up everything which the conjurer had expected to drop in the detective's lap, like some anarchist's bomb. He asked, 'What am I going to do? I will have to tell Mr Maskelyne about this, and it may result in the loss of my position.'

I asked, 'Are you not indispensible to Mr Maskelyne?' Holmes said, 'Watson *nobody* is indispensible. But Mr Devant, I feel that your employer is treading almost as dangerous a path himself.' Devant said, 'Ah, so you have seen the newspapers? The Guv'nor decided on that course and informed me soon after you and the doctor had left the hall. The Courier reporter was on the premises, concerning the murder and he went with J.N. in a hansom to De Kolta's home in Clerkenwell. What J.N. did may appear tasteless, but it makes me no more anxious to tell him about the ring.'

'Then do not immediately tell him, Mr Devant. Give

me a day, and I will try and regain the ring for you.'

As Devant put on his hat and picked up his coat he performed these actions as if he were taking his 'call' at the Egyptian Hall.

Britain's most charismatic conjurer left, I felt, a little less anxious than when he arrived. The slight tremor was still there, but barely noticeable when he shook hands with us. I remarked on it to Holmes, who said, 'I leave medical diagnosis to you Doctor.' I replied, 'Well, short of a proper examination I would suspect the early warning signs of "paralysis agitans".' We both remarked to the effect that we hoped my diagnosis could be incorrect.

It was by now, I felt, rather too late to suggest that Holmes should call Mrs Hudson for a late breakfast. In any case I could see that he was preparing to go out. As he lifted a hat and stick from the rack he said, 'Watson, I shall be very surprised if I do not return to Baker Street before this day is out, bearing Lady Windrush's ring. However, tell no one of my mission, especially Lestrade, should he materialise. Unless of course you would care to accompany me. I warn you, the enterprise may not be without its dangers.'

I was somewhat hurt by his words and said, warmly, 'You do not then consider it better to have an ex-army officer with you if danger is involved? I may have been wounded in Her Majesties' Service Holmes, but I am still no weakling!'

Holmes laughed in an open and wholesome manner. 'Watson, my dear friend, I was simply teasing you. There is no man in England that I would rather have at my side in a tight corner than your good self.'

I said, 'Right Holmes, I'm your man then, but I warn you that I shall insist on stopping somewhere for a late breakfast or early luncheon.'

Perhaps a half an hour later we were standing at a coffee stall near Middlesex Street, that gateway to the East End as one leaves the city itself. I had drawn the line at the 'pie and eel shop' which Holmes, with his cosmopolitan tastes, had been willing enough to patronise. But I was happy enough, aye hungry enough, to enjoy the bread and sausage and steaming mugs of coffee with which we refreshed ourselves.

I asked the obvious question. 'Why have you come to this particular area Holmes?' He spoke quietly, perhaps as a gentle hint to myself. 'Watson, I'll wager that the thief will want to unload that ring as quickly as humanly possible. Most of the "fences" for such a valuable item are within a stone's throw of where we stand. They are all known to me. Indeed I know of two or three who would be able to find the sort of money involved. It would be four thousand pounds if the thief knows what he has, and that is but a fraction of the real value. We will start first at the premises of a Mr Webber. He and I have met before.'

Webber's shop, which we reached via many back alleys, was a sort of bric-a-brac establishment. From outside it was all but impossible to see the wares through the glass of windows or door, so thick was the grime. Inside, every-thing: vases, books, furnishings and glassware, was cov-ered with what Mr Webber referred to as a 'lovely bloom'.

'My dear Mr Holmes, the customers won't touch anything these days unless it's got a lovely bloom. If it's too clean they fancy you are charging them its full value. They like to find something . . . dirty that they think is cheap and imagine they can clean up!' Mr Webber was a small, stout, round-faced man, wearing a kimono which might well have arrived at his premises from some auction sale of oriental articles. 'Mr Webber, I have a favour to ask.' 'Name it, it is yours my dear Mr Holmes. I haven't forgotten how you helped me over that little misunderstanding I had with the police . . .'

'You surrendered to me a very valuable necklace, that I might return it to its owner. In return I kept your name out of the affair. But of course Scotland Yard would still be interested in your activities.' Webber cast his eyes down, demurely, saying, 'That episode cost me a lot of money Mr Holmes . . . but worth it to retain the trust of a gentleman such as yourself.'

Holmes described the ring he was seeking. I had never thought him capable of blackmail before. 'If anyone has brought such a ring in to you I want to know about it. You would be surprised what I hear about Mr Webber, and should I learn that you took some part in this enterprise, Dartmoor will assuredly have a new inmate.'

Webber was grovelling now . . . 'Mr Holmes, you're not playing the game. I lost a fortune when I gave up that necklace. I haven't got that ring, I swear it. If I did I'd give it up to you. I prefer to deal with a gentleman like yourself rather than the bogeys, I swear I haven't got it.'

'Have you heard anything about it?'

'No, on my life . . .'

'Your life might be involved. It's a case of murder, and if you had anything to do with it . . .'

Webber breathed hard. 'All right Mr Holmes, if I tell you where you might and I did say *might*, find it, will you leave me out of any investigation? More, will you give me your word as a gentleman, and I know you to be just that, that you will not use that necklace business against me again?'

'If you give me some information, leading to a successful recovery, I will not tell anyone where I got my steer, and as far as you and I are concerned, the slate will be clean.'

Mr Webber printed something with a pencil stub on a scrap of paper. He folded it, gave it to Holmes, but he did not seem very happy.

Back in the mean alley Holmes opened the paper, and we saw the single word: STRINGER.

I asked, 'Do you know of this Stringer?' Holmes nodded, 'Oh yes, almost as well as I do Webber, in fact I know them all. But time is the essence and it would take days to go through my list. I think we struck lucky by visiting Webber.'

Holmes of course knew where Stringer's shop was, and I was grateful that I would not have to find my own way back through the maze of alleyways. Stringer's shop proved only a shade less dingy looking than had Webber's, and as we reached it, Holmes motioned for me to stop.

'Watson do you think you could give a convincing impersonation of a Scotland Yard man? After all, you have Lestrade as the perfect model. You have the military bearing which many police officers also have.' I agreed that such a charade might be possible. Holmes said, 'Good, then I will go into Stringer's shop. I intend to deal with him much as I did Webber. But if he has the ring it might be rather more difficult to get him to give it up. If I think he does not have it, I will be out within two or three minutes. If I think he has it I will be longer. If I do not emerge within five minutes I want you to burst into the shop, and "arrest" him. I rely on your good sense and acting ability from there on.' I promised to 'play my part'.

Five minutes is not long. There are twelve such periods in every hour and for most of us they pass rapidly. But given the circumstances that I have explained, it can seem like an hour. Every few seconds I looked at my watch, until that big hand threatened that 'witching diget'. Then as it became five minutes following Holmes' entry into

Stringer's, I burst in through the door. Holmes stood at the counter in converse with the man who had to be Stringer. He was a very tall man of about four and forty, with an elf-like face and dundreary whiskers. Assuming my most dignified bearing I marched up to the counter and dropping a hand on his shoulder barked out the words, in a fair imitation of Lestrade, 'Stringer, the game's up! I arrest you for the theft of a diamond ring, the property of Lady Windrush. Anything you say may be used against you in court!'

As I performed my part I dared not look at Holmes. He said nothing.

Stringer spoke in a thin weedy voice, and pleaded, 'Please Inspector, 'ave mercy on me. I'm just a poor dealer, I don't ever nick nuffin'!' Holmes said to me, 'Could there perhaps be some mistake Inspector? I said, 'None at all, I have my orders to arrest this man. You keep out of it.' Holmes rejoined warmly, 'I happen to be Sherlock Holmes, I'm a good friend of Inspector Lestrade. Surely if this poor man were to give you the ring you need say no more about it?' I said, 'Ooh, I don't know about that Mr Holmes, I've got my orders!'

Holmes, who should have been an actor, launched into his big speech. 'Look Inspector, this poor man is no thief and he bought the ring in good faith. But if he gives it up to you the loss will be his.'

I played up as I thought he wanted me to, 'It's more than my job is worth, we are making an example of receivers at the moment. Stringer will get fifteen years at least and hard labour at that.'

Suddenly Stringer 'broke'. He said, 'Please Inspector, pity a poor man with a wife and eight children to support!' He took some keys from below the counter and said, 'Wait, wait here . . . I'll get the ring.' We kept him in sight through the aperture which divided the shop from the back room and watched as he opened the safe. He returned with a magnificent diamond and ruby ring, the size and brilliance of which I had never seen before. I took it from him, looked at it carefully and passed it to my friend. Holmes examined it carefully and from his expression and manner I knew that it was indeed the Windrush ring. Then he confirmed it by saying, 'Look here Inspector, you have got your missing ring. Why not just take it and leave this poor fellow to repent, and remember the lesson he has undoubtedly learned.'

I said, 'I think I would require a little more. If he were to co-operate as far as I believe he is able . . .'

Holmes asked, 'Suppose Stringer were to describe the person from whom he obtained the ring?'

I said, 'Ah, now that might make a difference. Yes, I think that such information might well put a different complexion on the matter.'

Stringer looked positively hunted as he said, 'Mr Holmes is enough of a man of the world to know the danger that such collaboration would put me in!' I said, 'I too am a man of the world, enough at least to know that you will be breaking stones until 1913 if you don't give us every help!'

The receiver wrung his hands and looked about him furtively before saying 'All right gentlemen, I'm in between the devil and the deep so to speak. The bloke who brought in the ring, this very morning, was a rather tall fellow, but very slim. Couldn't see much of his face because he had a hat pulled well down in front. He was dressed roughly, and that's about all really . . .' He trailed off.

Gimlet-eyed, Holmes enquired, 'Hair colouring . . . complexion?' 'Well Sir, as I said he had this hat pulled well down, but I did notice a few wisps of reddish hair. What I could see of his face was rather pale. I suppose you would call it a fair complexion.' He looked uncertainly from Holmes to myself. Holmes shot me an obvious glance of enquiry. I shook my head grimly. This seemed to have the desired effect. Stringer said, 'His boots, I noticed his boots . . . They were brown, and good ones, too good for a man dressed as he was. His voice was low pitched, but I expect it was disguised . . .' He trailed off again.

Holmes passed the ring to me, and I took an envelope from my pocket and placed the ring inside it. Then I carefully placed the package into my inside jacket pocket. I was still making sure to keep up my impersonation of a Scotland Yard Inspector of Detectives! I said, 'Stringer, this is your lucky day. Had Mr Holmes not interceded on your behalf I would have arrested you and charged you with the crime of receiving. Be sure to keep out of trouble in the future!'

As we left the shop Stringer called after us, 'God Bless you Mr Holmes, and thank you kindly Inspector!' We both nodded curtly as we left.

Outside, we walked smartly away from Stringer's premises. Indeed it was not until we were about three hundred yards away that we dared to open our mouths. I think we both knew that near hysteria was imminent. It was Holmes who laughed first, and after that we had difficulty in pulling ourselves together. When we had recovered a little, Holmes said, 'Oh Watson, you really should have been a policeman, you do it so well. You have often said to me that my becoming a detective robbed the stage of a great actor. But how about yourself? Why Irving himself could not have bettered your performance.'

As I handed him the ring, still in its envelope, I asked Holmes, 'But why did you not enlist the help of the real police, once your suspicions were confirmed?' He replied, 'I believe I can be more help to Devant by taking this course. There is another reason, and before long you will know everything my dear Watson.'

I was a little hurt that he did not immediately take me into his confidence, but I knew from past experience that whenever Holmes kept me in the dark he did so for very good reasons. Certainly it had never been because my good sense or diplomacy was in doubt.

Holmes had, and has a sort of built in 'homing instinct', rather like a cat or homing-pigeon. He swiftly led the way through that labyrinth of tiny alleys and streets, so well described by Charles Dickens, particularly in 'Oliver Twist'. From the windows and around the walls there appeared living examples of the characters immortalised by Cruikshank.

When we we regained the comparative safety and sanity of the Commercial Road, Holmes raised his cane to hail a cab. We sank back into the comfort of its padded interior and gently travelled in the direction of Baker Street while I mused upon the fact that in this busy world the hansom represents escape. Once inside it, however mean the surroundings, you can close your eyes in the comforting knowledge that you will soon be home.

# CHAPTER FIVE

# 'The Grand Old Man'

'There is no peace for the wicked' is an oft repeated quotation and whilst it is one which I would not wish to apply to myself, I was reminded of it when Holmes announced . . . within minutes of our regaining the stability of 221b Baker Street . . . that we must attend the matinee at the Egyptian Hall. However, I absolutely insisted that we should partake of a luncheon first. Mrs Hudson was able to produce an excellent cut from the mutton joint, followed by a steaming suet pudding, annointed with a jugful of her famous custard. Then, as we toyed with the cheese and biscuits, once again I felt ready for anything.

'Come Doctor, we have placated the "inner man", and must resume our activities. There are two main reasons for this second visit to "Egypt in Piccadilly": the first to interview the famous Buatier De Kolta, the second to do what we should have done last night, and beard the lion in his den.'

I asked, 'You mean J.N. Maskelyne himself?'

'Exactly . . . the grand old man of magic!'

'Shall you hand over the ring to Devant?'

'Certainly not, although I shall certainly put his mind at rest upon the subject.'

'How about Lestrade?'

'The Inspector is investigating a murder, not a robbery. There will be a right time for him to learn everything . . . that is if it becomes necessary.'

When we arrived at the mysterious little theatre, Holmes purchased two rear stalls at the box office. The sort of seats which at a music hall would have been in 'The Pit'. I did not need to enquire as to why he did not simply present his card or mention Devant's name at the window, for whilst he had made no attempt at disguise (an art at which he is a past master), he was yet dressed in unsuitable clothes, of the kind which the working people might wear. Moreover he had bidden me to wear an equally unsuitable country tweed.

Thus 'subdued', we merged quite nicely with the other patrons of the less expensive seats and were able to view the performance without drawing undue attention from public or staff. As for that performance itself, it was much as we had seen before, except that there were some alterations in the order of presentation. A printed slip, inserted in the programme announced:

'Due to the sad demise of "Cyrano", his place will be taken at this performance by the famous continental illusionist, M. Buatier De Kolta.'

As it turned out, De Kolta's appearance occurred immediately before the interval. We watched his contribution with the very greatest interest.

With the passing of the years I cannot recall everything which transpired during De Kolta's performance, or indeed the exact order in which he presented his various wonders. But wonders they were. He made a wire birdcage containing a fluttering canary disappear between his large hands. He poured hundreds of colourful blooms from a paper cornucopia, and caused a substantial lady seated upon a chair to disappear from beneath a cloth. Despite his rather bizarre appearance (for he was ill-fitted in the matter of his evening clothes and untidily bearded with a wild mane of hair), he was much appreciated by the audience who could only gasp with astonishment at his various wonders. But it was his final item which really roused the audience. He presented his expanding cube, almost exactly as Cyrano had shown it.

I remarked to Holmes, 'His expanding cube appears very like that presented by Cyrano.' Holmes replied, 'Not only very like, but exactly like. It is probably the same apparatus, for do you not remember that De Kolta declared last night he had not finished building the illusion?'

I had to agree that I remembered that statement.

During the intermission we emerged from the front of the building and passed into the side street to seek the stage door. This aperture was guarded by an elderly retainer whose job it was to check all arrivals and departures.

'Might I ask who you two gents are? We don't 'old with no stage door Johnny's 'ere yer know! Try the Empire!' His tone was sardonic, surly and unwholesome, like his appearance. He wore a velveteen jacket, from which a bottle of spirits could be seen emerging. Upon his head he wore a flat artisan's cap, not unlike that sported by Holmes. As for his trousers, these could not be seen due to a closed half door over which he leered, like some punchinello in a booth. He held a newspaper at arms' length.

'My name is Holmes, and my colleague's name is Watson.'

' 'olmes eh . . . not *Sherlock* 'olmes? I don't fink . . .'

'The very same, now if you would inform Mr Devant of our arrival . . .'

'Mr Devant is a very busy man and he relies upon my discretion as to 'oo I admits and 'oo I doesn't.' He ingratiatingly drew the back of his right hand across his mouth, insinuating that the price of a drink might admit us. Holmes leaned forward, his prominent nose almost touching that of the stage door keeper . . .

'Now listen my man, I make some allowance for the fact that you have been in a bar room brawl, during the course of which your spectacles were broken. But if you do not summon Mr Devant immediately I will be forced to suggest to him that he dismiss you at the earliest possibility. You will drink little "Engine Eightpenny" without a weekly wage! So stir yourself, or you'll be packed off back to Hackney directly!'

The uncouth fellow's jaw had dropped. He asked, ' 'ow joo know I come from 'ackney?' Holmes smiled sweetly at him. 'Your own unmistakable version of the London dialect tells me that, and the smell of "Engine Eight-penny" is unmistakable too.' He looked glum, saying, 'Well 'ow didja know about the fight, and me breakin' me glasses?' I was wondering about that too. Holmes said, 'The scar upon the bridge of your nose indicates that you habitually wear spectacles. The newspaper in your hand, held at arms' length indicates their loss. A bar room brawl was the most likely circumstance for the breakage.'

The uncouth fellow pulled a cork from a speaking tube,

which he blew down, unmusically, to attract the attention of whoever was at its other end. 'Mr 'olmes and some doctor to see Mr Devant, Charlie!' Then he waved us past him with a gruff gesture, saying, 'Through the doors and on the right.'

Ever the gentleman, Devant awaited us beyond the doors and following the usual pleasantries he said, 'You should have given your name at the box office . . .' But Holmes interrupted, 'We preferred to merge into the background, as you will see from our attire. I was particularly intrigued with Mr De Kolta's performance, and especially the inclusion of the illusion which has been a bone of contention. After all, by his own admission this had not progressed beyond the planning stage.'

Devant replied, 'He is using Cyrano's model with our blessing. No relative has stepped forward to claim his effects, and Madame Patricia proved willing to participate. There seems little doubt that Cyrano pirated the illusion, so this outcome seems a fair one.'

Then Holmes dropped his 'bombshell'.

'I have recovered the Windrush ring, Mr Devant. Or rather, Doctor Watson has!'

I blushed at this mention of my small part in the affair. But Devant seemed delighted to say the very least. At first his excitement was such that he could not respond to the good news. Eventually he said, 'I cannot thank either of you enough. God Bless you Mr Holmes, Doctor Watson! Should I contact Her Ladyship?'

'No, I will return the ring to her myself, and I must extract one promise from you before the matter can be laid to rest, if indeed it can.'

'You have but to name it sir.'

'Despite your earlier plans you must promise to observe

a silence as far as the news reporters are concerned. Her Ladyship would *not* appreciate publicity concerning the affair.'

Devant coloured slightly. 'But . . . but Mr Holmes . . . the Windrush ring is world-famous, and the publicity would be invaluable!'

Holmes said, 'Even so!' Devant paused before he replied, 'Very well, you have my word.'

I could see that Devant's joy at the return of the ring was tempered by the fact that he could not take full advantage theatrically. Holmes asked, 'May we perhaps see Mr Maskelyne? You have my assurance that the ring will not be mentioned.'

The so-called 'Grand Old Man' proved to be younger than this term of endearment or stage image suggested. A man, I judged, of perhaps five years beyond his half century, he was of spare build, and sported a rather large moustache, a drooping affair usually known as a 'walrus'. This and his drooping eyelids gave him a rather mournful appearance. But his movements were sprightly, as one would expect of a man who nightly caused a dozen dinner plates to 'waltz'.

'My dear Holmes, I have long looked forward to meeting you and your distinguished "Boswell". I understand that you are making some private enquiries regarding this terrible tragedy surrounding poor Cyrano?'

He seated us comfortably enough, yet this vast attic room had not the order or comfort of Devant's lair. It was for the most part a vast workshop with portions of partially dismembered automata everywhere. Strange glass-eyed mannikins gazed fixedly from hooks upon the wall, and most of the floor space was occupied by cabinets and boxes decorated with mysterious hieroglyphics. A work bench occupied one wall, covered with wood and steel working implements.

A miniature turbanned Turk sat cross-legged atop a glass pillar. Maskelyne gestured towards it. 'Psycho . . . my most famous creation!'

'Retired?' I jested.

'No, simply resting.' He took my jest at its face value.

I could not help but notice that Maskelyne had the room arranged as if he were used to keeping visitors at arms length from his inventions. Holmes asked, 'You were in this room at the time of the tragedy Mr Maskelyne?' 'Yes, I spend most of my time here when not actually upon the stage. The running of the hall I leave to young Devant and this gives me the time I need to work upon my inventions. Before he joined me I used to use the dressing room in which poor Cyrano met his end.'

Holmes asked, 'And your automata?'

'There is a room next to that dressing room which can be more than securely locked. I keep my "secretary" automata there at present, because it is near to the stage.'

'May we be taken into that room sir?'

Maskelyne was not delighted at Holmes' request, I could see. But he did not lose his composure, and said, 'If you deem it absolutely necessary Mr Holmes?' The detective nodded and Maskelyne took a key from a hook on the wall. We followed him down the stairs.

I noticed that Maskelyne turned the key several times in order to open the lock on the door next to Cyrano's dressing room. 'It is my own invention, it would take considerable skill to pick it. I may patent the lock.'

The room was almost bare except for the stenographic automata. Holmes studied the mechanical wonder with acute interest. 'May I be permitted a view of the inner mechanism?' Maskelyne, a little reluctant, opened a panel to reveal a series of cogs and levers. Holmes looked at them keenly. 'Ah yes, most ingenius!'

Maskelyne seemed happier once the panel was closed. Holmes glanced around the room, but there was little else of interest to him. He opened the cupboard which corresponded with that in Cyrano's room. Then closing it again he smiled disarmingly at Maskelyne and said, 'Well I do not believe that there is much in here to capture our attention. I am sorry to have put you to this inconvenience Mr Maskelyne. We need keep you from your work no longer.'

Maskelyne relocked the door as carefully as he had unlocked it, and, with his friendly manner restored, bade us good day. 'Devant will see to your wishes and requirements Mr Holmes. He has so much more a finger on the pulse than I.'

As the 'Grand Old Man' made his exit, leaving us standing in the corridor, one of the white-faced clowns, still in his full motley, appeared on the scene. He almost grovelled as Maskelyne passed him. Then he turned to us and said, 'If you're the new stage hands you want to steer clear of *that* room . . . He pointed to the door which Maskelyne had just locked. 'It's haunted! Why, when the old man had the dressing room next door, several of the artistes heard voices coming from that room when it was known to be empty! Strange noises too!'

The clown scampered off toward his dressing room, and I glanced at Holmes to see if he considered the information from our capering informant to be of importance. He returned my glance with raised eyebrows and a shrug, and in that clairvoyant manner of his, remarked, 'Maybe Watson, maybe. But that which I saw within the room was of more interest than any number of ghost stories!'

Holmes knocked politely upon the door of the dressing room which had been Cyrano's, but now bore a paper name plate, 'Buatier De Kolta'.

'Entree, entree . . .' We entered as bidden but the continental illusionist, who looked still very untidy in his street clothes, politely addressed us in English, 'Mr Detective and good Doctor, please to come in. This is my assistant, yes, Matthew Craig.'

He introduced a tall man in early middle-age, with a very distinctive quiff. He was spare of figure and had a thin face, rather like Holmes.

De Kolta was not backward in speaking to us upon the subject which was on all our minds. 'I admit I did threaten Cyrano, but I spoke, how you say, in the hotness of the moment? Why even the good Inspector seems happy on that matter, and Maskelyne would not at once have thought of me had he not decided on my innocence.'

Holmes spoke, as if assuming De Kolta's innocence. 'I am more interested in how Cyrano pipped you to the post with the "expanding cube".' The illusionist said, 'It is a mystery! I only had plans and a working model, but he was actually able to produce the illusion!'

I could not help thinking that even Holmes was getting a little out of his depth. Was a murder investigation not enough for him without the complication of stolen secrets of illusion? Especially as he had only been brought on the scene to find a missing ring, which he had already found. But as these thoughts passed through my mind, my eyes and ears detected Holmes questioning Matthew Craig.

'I imagine that the piracy of the expanding cube must have bothered you quite a lot Mr Craig. As a long standing retainer of Mr De Kolta you must have felt the loss almost as keenly as he did?'

'Oh yes, and my anger was almost as great. Mr De Kolta has been very good to me since we first met on a fairground in Vienna.'

'You were working on the fairground?'

'That's right, I was an acrobat, but reduced to appearing with freaks, dwarfs, dog-faced people and the like. However, I also made and decorated all the facades and properties for the sideshow, and Mr De Kolta recognised my talent. He makes the rough models and I make the finished ilusions.'

Holmes nodded with evident interest and when he noticed a portfolio upon a high shelf, he asked, 'Is that your album Mr De Kolta?' 'Why no, I imagine it was left there, it probably belonged to Cyrano . . . that rascal . . .'

Holmes reached for the article. I knew it was within his grasp or just beyond but even though he could reach it, he feigned an inability to do so. 'Mr Craig, do you think you could reach the album and hand it to me?'

Craig, who was about the same height and reach as Holmes, gained it with ease. However, I noticed that in so doing he dislocated his shoulder, and just as quickly returned that member to its normal position. He handed the portfolio to Holmes who, I felt sure, had noticed the unusual movement.

Holmes flicked through the book, and announced, 'It appears to be Cyrano's scrap book. Evidently Inspector Lestrade has overlooked it. There would seem to be little harm in my borrowing and studying it.'

We all nodded our assent.

Before leaving the Hall, we looked in on Devant in his lair. I had assumed that Holmes simply wanted to bid him goodnight, and perhaps to thank him for his cooperation.

But the detective had a request to make. 'Mr Devant, do you think you could forgo your cantor on Hampstead Heath tomorrow morning, and rendezvous with me here at seven?' A somewhat puzzled Devant agreed to this.

That night we sat comfortably in the living room at Baker Street, partaking of the succulent snacks provided by Mrs Hudson, the hour being rather late for dinner. Afterwards, Holmes filled a pipe which he lit with a Vespa. I enquired, 'One last smoke before bed eh?' My friend informed me that he had Cyrano's scrapbook to study first. He transferred himself to the table, where he spread open the volume and carefully studied its contents. From my armchair I could see that it contained those items which you would expect an actor's press book to hold: newspaper cuttings, interspersed with tipped-in theatre programmes and photographic portraits.

Suddenly Holmes extended a hand toward me and demanded, 'Watson, be so kind as to pass my lens!'

For reasons that I could not imagine the lens was on the mantelpiece. Somewhat reluctantly I rose from the comfort of my chair, took up the lens and handed it to my friend. He used it to peer at a large photograph which depicted a number of performers outside a booth, upon a platform. Even with the naked eye I could pick out the central figure which clearly, and not surprisingly turned out to be Cyrano. He was holding a paper cornucopia from which peered a white rabbit. He looked younger, as indeed did Madame Patricia at his side. To the left there was a group of small people who appeared to be dwarfs. Holmes handed me the lens and asked me to tell him what I could see.

I looked again, this time through the lens. I said, 'Cyrano, Madame Patricia, and some dwarfs . . .' He interrupted, 'Midgets, not dwarfs, for see how perfectly proportioned they are despite their Lilliputian size. What else?'

I peered again through the lens. 'Some sort of large poster or banner, depicting a contortionist. It reads "The Fellow in the Flask", and . . . by jove, I do believe it is Matthew Craig!'

'Exactly! So he and Cyrano were acquainted, and Craig was a contortionist as well as a gymnast. I had suspected as much when he dislocated his shoulder to reach that high shelf. This business is rather more complex than I had imagined Watson.'

Tired by the day's activities, within half an hour I was quite ready for bed. Before retiring I said, 'I would advise you to try and get some sleep Holmes, if you are to meet Devant at seven.' Then I added, a little accusingly, 'As you have said nothing, I assume I am not to accompany you tomorrow?'

Holmes turned upon me his most enigmatic expression as he said, 'My dear Watson, even such a competent gentleman as yourself can hardly be in two places at once!' I said, 'But I have no plans for tomorrow.' He said, 'Oh but you have Watson, or rather I have plans for you.' I dared to ask, 'Might I enquire as to their nature?'

Holmes closed the portfolio, and put down the lens. Then taking up his Turkish slipper, he recharged his pipe. As he filled it I glared at him, knowing how he loved to keep me in suspense. But he spared me waiting until he had lit it and said, 'Someone, and someone that I can trust completely, will have to return Lady Windrush's ring. As you know, I have not the time to journey to Sussex myself.'

I was not too sure if I should feel flattered with the seeming importance of the errand or put out by the thought of being a courier or Jack of all trades. After all, Holmes had assumed automatically that I would undertake the mission without question. He must have read my mind, for with the skill of a 'Zanzig', he said, 'The ring is worth many thousands of pounds Watson. Who could any man trust with such a mission except his dearest friend? You are my dearest friend Watson . . . come to think of it, my *only* friend!'

It was very like Holmes to issue a compliment with a sting in its tail. What could I say but, 'Very well Holmes, I will look up the trains for Haywards Heath at once. That is, I believe the nearest railway station to Windrush Towers?'

'That is correct Watson. I have been in contact with Lady Windrush. You may possibly have noticed a crested envelope among my letters? Her Ladyship has requested me to keep the whole matter from the attention of the police and newspapers. So far, this has been possible. But just how long I can keep up this confidence I am not sure. So you see, the matter is a delicate one.'

# CHAPTER SIX

# Windrush Towers

---

The bustle of Victoria Station has always fascinated me. The great number of people arriving, full of excitement at the thought of a visit to the Zoological Gardens, or the Tower of London. Then there are the hordes who descend upon the station in the summer months, bound for Brighton, Worthing and other resorts, clutching buckets and spades and wicker hampers filled with comestibles. The air is often unbearably filled with the fretful cries of over-excited children and the laments of elderly persons who have lost either their baggage or their train . . .

I did not await my train in the apartment designated for that purpose: rather in the comparative comfort of a vast refreshment hall, with its marble columns and steaming urns. It has been said that if one were able to sit long enough in such a place one would eventually see almost everyone that one had known, assuming that they were still in the land of the living. I partook of a cup of coffee and a Chelsea bun, which for their price were good enough, although the china cup was a little on the thick side (which I find dulls the taste). Thence to the bookstall to purchase a newspaper and a copy of 'The Strand', and at last I was able to sink back in the tolerable comfort of a first-class carriage.

Although empty when I entered it, alas, before the train started, my carriage was invaded by a rather wild-looking man with a bush of hair and a demoniacal expression. I was about to go to the trouble of changing carriages when the whistle blew, the guard waved his flag, and I realized I had left it too late. I felt sure that the bizarre fellow did not have a first-class ticket and said as much. He leaned toward me from the opposite seat and said, 'Ticket? I don't need a ticket! You see, I am the German Kaiser, here on a special mission.'

There followed one of the most terrifying half hours that I have ever spent. The fellow was clearly both demented and dangerous, and I had omitted to bring my service revolver with me. He started to march up and down between the seats, causing me to hastily withdraw my feet. He leaned out of the carriage window, shouting 'Deuchland Uber Alles!' He had some 'secret plans' for the destruction of Buckingham Palace, which he insisted on showing to me. There was no way in which even an experienced medical man like myself could judge if he would become violent, as such lunatics (sometimes said to have the 'strength of ten'), quite often do. For the first time that I could remember I found myself wishing that I had taken one of those irritating trains which stop at every town, village and hamlet.

At long last the train shuddered to a stop at a village called Three Bridges and the door of the carriage opened to admit a railway official. 'All tickets please!' he demanded. As I always do in such situations I thought quickly and said, 'Ticket Inspector, please pay attention to this fellow here, he has been behaving wildly and claims that he is going to blow up Buckingham Palace!'

By one of those miracle transformations that only the cunning of a lunatic seems able to produce, the strange fellow had smoothed back his hair and reverted his facial expression to one of extreme normality. He sat quietly, reading *my* copy of 'The Strand'. The ticket inspector said, 'We've had a warning to look out for an escaped patient from the asylum.' The lunatic pointed to me and said, in a quiet, pleasant voice, 'There is your man Inspector, he's been behaving wildly since we left Victoria. Furthermore, he has had the audacity to steal my ticket!'

The inspector asked for my ticket and demanded to know my name. I said, 'Certainly, here is my ticket, a first-class one to Haywards Heath, and my name is John H. Watson, colleague and confidente of Sherlock Holmes, the famous Baker Street detective!'

I thought that I had played a trump card, but evidently I had not. The lunatic laughed merrily and held open the 'The Strand' at the page where commenced one of my accounts of Holmes' adventures. He shrugged as to 'rest his case'. The uncouth inspector dragged me to my feet, out of the carriage and onto the platform. 'Unhand me! I'll have you know that I am on an extremely delicate mission for Mr Holmes!' A station-boy grabbed my arm, twisting it behind my back, as the train door was slammed shut, and the whistle and flag sent it speeding toward my intended destination.

I am a very tolerant man but I confess that at this point I lost my temper.

'I have an important appointment at Haywards Heath!' I insisted. The inspector nodded wisely, 'Very true sir, they have a very famous asylum there.'

Of course, in the fullness of time the misunderstanding was settled. I was taken to the station master's office, where that worthy, having looked at my card and listened to my story, issued me with a hand written 'emergency ticket' and sent me on my way with his apologies. But I had a long time to wait for another train, and I knew that I would be late in keeping my appointment.

The rest of my journey was mercifully uneventful until I secured a cab outside the station at Haywards Heath. To call it a 'cab' is hardly accurate. The shoddy equipage, horse and driver, were not of a standard that could have plied for hire in London.

'Where to Squire?' The driver was over-familiar in his manner, and before I could reply he had added, 'Is it the asylum?' I said, 'Certainly not, take me to Windrush Towers without delay, I'm in a hurry!'

The horse managed a fast walk . . . I can hardly refer to it as a trot, and after some time we arrived outside the entrance of a large and rather run-down country house. For his rudeness I gave the cabby his exact fare. He looked at the coins in his hand and said, 'Don't ask me to come back for yer!' I replied, 'Certainly not, Lady Windrush will doubtless have me driven to the station!' He laughed sardonically and his vehicle left as fast as his horse could walk.

I was admitted to Windrush Towers by a very elderly retainer who all but creaked as he walked. I diagnosed, without examination of course, advanced arthritis and slight senility. Having taken my hat and cane, he ushered me to the open double doors of a large reception room. I could see at its far end a handsome woman in a silk gown, her right hand resting upon the jewelled collar of a female mastiff.

Prompted by my calling card, the senile retainer shouted, 'Doctor John H. Watson!' Then in a rather hoarse whisper he said to me, 'Look out Cully, she's a man-eater!'

I was taken aback, until I realised that he must be referring to the dog. Indeed as I entered, the mastiff started such a growling and barking as I have seldom heard. The retainer took it out of the room, with a considerable struggle. As the noise of its barking gradually subsided, Lady Windrush spoke.

'Doctor Watson, so nice of you to come. I get so few visitors.' 'A pleasure dear lady, I know that my colleague, Mr Sherlock Holmes, has informed you of the purpose of my visit, the return of your ring?'

She patted the embroidered cushion on a chair, as if directing a pet dog to 'sit'. As I collapsed onto the Chippendale she said, 'Of course, and I was so delighted when I got his wire. I had as a matter of fact expected you earlier, but I expect you had trouble with the trains, such wretched things.'

She was an attractive lady of about eight and thirty, comely of shape, and exquisitely dressed in a silk dress of great complexity. She had chestnut hair, piled upon her head, lightly flecked with grey. To my inexpert eyes, her cosmetic arrangements seemed to be a bit on the heavy side.

I told her the story of the lunatic, and her sympathies were profound. She poured me a glass of some excellent port and received the ring with delight. 'Dear Doctor, you have saved my life . . . well, at least, you have spared me a very great embarrassment. You see (she recharged my glass without being prompted), my husband gave me the ring about ten years ago. It cost him something like ten thousand pounds. It is a very famous ring with a long history. The exact arrangement of the diamonds and rubies is unique. It is illustrated in all the reference works on the subject.' She hesitated, as if about to tell me something. I said, 'You can rely on my discretion Lady Windrush.'

She looked at me with a tremble of the lip and moisture in the eye and said, 'Of course, I trust you completely. You see, just a few years back there was a man with whom I had a clandestine friendship. Then a little later he threatened to tell my husband about it, unless I gave him a large amount of money.'

I started and all but rose in my chair, 'The blackguard!'

She continued, 'I realise that I take a risk in telling you this, but I am so desperate. I have explained that it was blackmail. There was no way that I could meet his demands, without asking my husband for the money, which of course I could not do. So I did a really dreadful thing. I had a good friend, a jeweller, whom I knew I could trust. He had the ring copied for me with far less expensive stones and he broke down the original ring and sold the stones for me.'

I could not believe what I was hearing and said, 'But you have worn the copy since and no-one has noticed the difference?'

'Amazingly, no! The piece is so well documented that it can be recognised at a glance. Moreover the copy is made from stones that are genuine, just far less valuable. So it would fool an expert.'

I took the ring in the tiny box in which we had placed it, and put it on the wine table beside her. I said, 'But Lady Windrush, after the unfortunate affair at Maskelyne's Theatre . . .' She interrupted, 'I wish I had never been to the wretched place. If the original ring had been involved I would have sued Maskelyne by now.'

'Even so, you went there and the ring disappeared as part of a conjurer's publicity scheme. But that scheme went wrong with the ring being stolen, by a man who may well have committed murder. He evidently took it to a receiver, from whom we managed to regain it. Before you explain, my next question would have been how did the thief fool the fence?'

She said, 'The fence doubtless recognised the setting, and then cut glass with the ring. I just thank God it's back, for I could not have told my husband Sir Percival that it was "being cleaned" indefinitely. I have you and your friend to thank for my deliverance, dear Doctor.'

She leaned forward to fill my glass, and had I not known her to be the lady that she undoubtedly is, I could have sworn that she leaned over a little further than was strictly necessary. She said, 'You will, both of you, be able to keep the matter from the police and newspapers, will you not dear Doctor Watson?' And she turned upon me such a 'little girl in trouble' expression that I was forced to say, 'Dear lady, I will do my very best to be discreet.'

The port was excellent, the afternoon was warm, and I felt a little faint. This was doubtless a threatened recurrence of the malaria fever from which I had suffered. I believe I may even have nodded off for a moment or two, and when I came to myself again, Lady Windrush was tidying her hair. She said, 'Dear John (I'm sure I may thus address you), now *I know* that you will do your best to keep the matter of my ring quiet.'

Our business concluded, there followed a pleasant enough half hour, during which Lady Windrush showed me portraits in her family album. There were many portraits of Sir Percival, stripped to the waist, in pugilistic poses. For variety there were some of him in wrestling leotards, the lady explaining that Sir Percival was possibly one of the finest wrestlers and middle-weight boxers in the country.

'Perhaps you will be able to stay for dinner? Percival is in the city today, but he will be back later and I know he would love to meet you. Of course we cannot mention the true reason for your visit, but we could say that you were here to examine me. You are a doctor, after all!'

It was then that I suddenly realised that I had been away from Baker Street far too long, and that for all I knew Holmes might be expecting me to support him in some exploit or other. I explained, 'Dear lady, much as I would love to accept your invitation, I really must depart. My friend, Mr Sherlock Holmes, relies upon my assistance with most of his activities. Moreover, our housekeeper, Mrs Hudson, prefers that I keep strictly to meal times.'

As the elderly retainer helped me into a dog-cart, I glanced back to the front entrance of Windrush Towers, where Lady Windrush, reunited with her mastiff bitch, stood, beautifully posed, with one hand resting upon its huge slavering head.

'Farewell dear Doctor, I look forward to our next meeting!' She waved a long silk cravat as the vehicle negotiated the gravel drive.

The return train journey to Victoria was rather uneventful, except that I fancied one or two people seemed to recognise me. Anyway, they looked at me and smiled, or else remarked to each other. And at Victoria the cabby, who took me to Baker Street winked at me hugely.

Mrs Hudson, unbidden, brought me some steaming hot coffee, and advised me to drink it black. 'Works wonders Doctor, you'll see!' I sometimes think that perhaps her retirement might be considered.

I was about to go to my bedroom, to freshen myself,

when my ablutions were interrupted by the return of Sherlock Holmes. I noticed that he carried the large carpet bag, in which he kept his disguises. He looked at me keenly.

'My dear Watson, I notice that you have had some dalliance with a lady. Her height would be about five and a half feet and her hair auburn, with the slightest hint of grey. Do not look so surprised, for you have rouge upon your face, and your lapel bears some auburn tresses. Oh, yes, and you have partaken liberally of forty year old port wine!'

I felt somewhat foolish and could only say, 'By jove, was it as old as all that?'

Holmes looked at me with, I felt, mock severity. 'Watson, I sent you on an important errand concerning a valuable diamond ring, not to dally with a married woman, and a titled one at that!'

I told Holmes everything that had occurred since I had last seen him, including the episode with the lunatic on the train, and the fullest details of my meeting and conversation with Lady Windrush. Eventually I reached the point when I dropped what I had thought was my bombshell, and gave him the information concerning the imitation status of the famous diamond ring. To my surprise my friend simply nodded wisely.

'I was aware that the ring was an imitation of the original, albeit an extremely clever one and made from real though far less valuable stones. It was clever enough a fake to take in a hardened jewel fence, so it is indeed a splendid replica. but the known character of the setting must have aided in the deception.'

I came to a delicate request. 'Holmes, do you think it will be possible to continue to keep the whole episode of the ring from the eyes and ears of the police and the newspapers?'

He turned upon me this time a look of real severity. 'My dear Watson, you have made Lady Windrush no promise to that effect I trust? Ah, I see from your expression that you have! Upon my word Watson, you had no right to do that. Now perhaps you can understand why I find it necessary to stand completely aloof to the wiles of women? You would be well advised to do the same whilst acting for me.'

Perhaps the forty year old port had made me bold. I said, 'Come Holmes, I would remind you of that affair of "Scandal in Bohemia". Did you not allow your admiration for a woman, Irene Adler, to affect your judgement and indeed your actions in the matter?'

He selected a pipe, a meersham, and charged it, tamped it and lit it before he replied. I noticed the veins at his forehead working, and regretted what I had said. However, I believe it was Confucious who once remarked, 'Twenty teams of oxon cannot withdraw a remark, once it has been made.' After what seemed an age, Holmes looked me squarely in the eyes and said, 'My dear Watson, that was unworthy of you. I thought you were friend enough to understand my dilemma of that time. Had I not been solely dedicated to pure, clear and positive thought, and avowed to follow my vocation rather as a monk does his, unhindered by such entanglements, I could have loved her. I say "could" you will note, because I was then and am now, dedicated to the way of life that I have chosen. She was a fine woman, *the* woman, I do not wish you to compare my admiration for Irene Adler with your flirtation with a woman who merely tried to use you to gain her selfish ends!'

I said nothing. I was full of anger, sorrow, regret and sheer hurt.

It was Holmes who next spoke.

'My apologies Watson, I have been harsh with you my dear fellow, more than harsh. You are a fine and very human person, a man with all the natural characteristics of a really noble gentleman, which you undoubtedly are. Of course you felt sorry for this seemingly frail and troubled woman. Let me say this: I will do all in my power to help you to keep your promise to her, however misguided it may have been. In fact I count it as a half-promise, for your good nature has been taken advantage of.'

I hardly knew how to reply for I felt wretched. My minor infidelity and over consumption of port had almost cost me the friendship of the wisest and finest man I have ever known. I had been cruel in bringing up an episode left to lie. Such is Holmes' nobility of character that he has never held my cruel outburst against me.

Although our friendship was mercifully intact there was yet a long silence before more was said. I broke it first by saying, unwisely perhaps, 'What sort of a day have you had Holmes?'

He chuckled and said, 'Good old Watson, the only ray of predictability in a world of confusion. I have had a very constructive day, I thank you. I met Devant at seven of the clock this morning, as arranged, and he took me onto the roof of the hall, where he makes his "films", as he calls them, for presentation as "animated photographs". I now have at least a tyro's knowledge of the principles involved.'

Although I did not say so, I felt that this thirst for knowledge regarding that which has since become known as 'Cine-photography' was a little misplaced. Were there not other more pressing matters worthy of his thought and study? What I actually asked was, 'Have Lestrade or yourself made any progress in the matter of the murder of poor Cyrano?'

He replied, 'You mean have I done anything else today beside playing around with a moving picture camera? Well, for your information I have again interviewed all those who might conceivably have had opportunity to commit the crime.'

'Madame Patricia, although not herself of sufficient strength to have committed such a violent act, couldn't entirely be ruled out as far as collusion was concerned.'

'So you questioned her?'

'Yes, very fully, particularly concerning those early fairground days of which we became aware through study of the scrapbook. She admitted that he was a man of uncertain temper and did not always see eye to eye with his fellow artistes. He had a violent quarrel with a midget, perhaps one of those depicted in the photograph.'

I wanted to hear more of his interviews with those whom we had considered more likely candidates for the role of murderer. I asked, 'Did you speak with De Kolta?'

'Yes, a charming if somewhat eccentric gentleman. He has the required strength and indeed the motive. But he could not have entered through the window, with his broad build. Craig, on the other hand could have dislocated his body to negotiate the window if, indeed that means of entrance was employed. His strength might have been sufficient to have committed the crime, for he has carpenter's hands and we know that he was acquainted with Cyrano, through the photograph.'

'Does he deny knowing Cyrano?'

'No, but he has not volunteered the information, which I find interesting. Of course he may be trying simply to avoid implication.'

'Who else did you question?'

'The elder Maskelyne, but he was somewhat put out by the loss of a tool from his workshop, some sort of calliper. He could not spare me much of his time. As far as I can establish he was in his eyrie at the time when Cyrano was killed. His son, Nevil, entered the room next to Cyrano's dressing room to place the automata there, not long before our estimated time for the crime. He heard nothing suspicious.'

'Did you speak with the clown with the whitened face?'

'I did, but the fellow seems to be a little limited intellectually. What in your inimitable style you would refer to as "ten pence in the shilling" Watson. He repeated those strange beliefs that the room where the automata is kept is haunted.'

'And the pickpocket fellow?'

'An interesting man, an American. He even gave me some lessons in the art of the "artful dodger"! I may write a monograph on this interesting subject.'

I laughed, 'Pickpockets are born, surely?'

Holmes smiled, with mischief in his eyes. 'Oh I don't know Watson, a little earlier I managed to deprive you of your watch and your wallet. Perhaps you would like them back?'

I felt for the articles that he had mentioned and experienced that moment of panic which their absence was sure to produce. My nimble fingered friend returned my property to me with a flourish. I said, 'Upon my word Holmes, you are incorrigible!'

And so, as Samuel Pepys would have said, 'To bed'.

# CHAPTER SEVEN

# Pathology and Horology

Breakfast at 221b on the following morning was reasonably uneventful by the standards of the last few days. Of course for an individual like myself this was to the good. Yet a part of me hoped that order would not reign. I had also to consider my friend, his breakdown of the previous year and the detrimental effect that inactivity might have upon him in the future. I thanked my maker for giving him work to do with his brilliant mind. There were two pressing matters for him to be concerned with: the Windrush diamond ring and the terrible murder of our poor client, Cyrano the illusionist, also known as Cyril Randolph.

'What are your plans for today Holmes?' I enquired. He replied, 'They have been made for me Watson, for a message from Lestrade requests that I rendezvous with him at the scene of the post-mortem. Not a jolly experience, and I would appreciate your support. After all, as a medical man you are more accustomed to such things.'

He was of course right in a literal sense, for I could not count the cadavers I had been forced to inspect. But from my experience, Holmes always seemed considerably less affected than I by such scenes. I have never quite gained that ideal detachment.

Lestrade pointed vaguely at the poor body on the slab with just that familiarity that does indeed breed contempt. Over the body crouched an elderly, silver-haired man in a bloodstained medical gown.

Lestrade introduced us, 'Mr Holmes, Dr Watson, this is Sir Bertram Staines, who has been conducting this post-mortem.' We nodded respectfully but did not offer to shake the hand that held the scalpal.

Sir Bertram spoke, 'You see Holmes, detectives as talented as yourself and the Inspector can be mistaken.' Holmes said, 'Certainly in my case Sir Bertram. My Boswell here does not document my mistakes and failures.'

The pathologist continued, 'My first thought was that the poor fellow had been very brutally strangled by some assailant with very large hands and enormous strength, which was I understand, your own conclusion. However, careful examination reveals that those equidistant discolourations have been caused by some powerful tool or implement, like some very large serrated calliper.'

Holmes and I, on closer inspection, could quite take his point. No fingers could have been quite so evenly placed.

Lestrade asked, 'What manner of trade could such a calliper be used for? I don't believe I have ever come across anything of the sort.'

Holmes said, 'Could it perhaps be some sort of calliper for adjusting a mechanism. For example, clockwork? Maskelyne tells me that he has lost a hand tool. Perhaps you could check upon its nature Lestrade?'

The Scotland Yard man sent a constable to Maskelyne's

Theatre. Holmes said, 'You see, more failure on my part Sir Bertram. I knew about the missing tool, but in my mind I dismissed any importance that it might have . . .'

The pathologist confirmed my on the spot diagnosis of a fractured vertebra. 'Whoever used this calliper on the deceased certainly used considerable strength, and threw him like a terrier with a rat.'

For the next half hour Sir Bertram gave us a very complete list of his findings. Cyril Randolph, we had known as a brilliant stage conjurer. The little more that we knew had been gleaned from photographs, press-cuttings and the oral statements of those who had known him. But the pathologist gave facts and not opinion.

'What we have here is the body of a well nourished man of about forty years of age. His height was exactly five feet eleven inches. He had no serious ailments and aside from a small patch of nervous eczema, was in good health. he spent a great deal of his life following occupations which required him to stand for long periods, illustrated by a tendency to varicose veins in the legs.'

Holmes was, I could see, most impressed. He tried to draw the pathologist to be a little more daring in his diagnosis. 'You didn't see him in life Sir Bertram, but can you deduce anything about his character from the body?'

Sir Bertram looked shrewdly at Holmes and said, 'He was a man more concerned with his outward appearance than his actual physical condition. Note the neatly cut hair and expertly trimmed whiskers. This and the carefully manicured hands contrast strangely with the overgrown and slightly calcified toenails. Until they actually caused him pain he would put on his boots and ignore the problem. The stains at the back of his teeth indicate that he was a cigar smoker, a moderate one. He had his appendix removed some years ago. The size of the scar indicates that he had neglected to have it attended to until forced by danger. So we have a man who would put off taking even important decisions until forced to.'

Holmes turned to me and said, 'Come Watson, here is a man after my own heart!'

The pathologist smiled and said, 'Our occupations follow similar lines and patterns. We observe and interpret, through our experience.'

After leaving the mortuary we spoke at some length with Lestrade. The inspector was forced to admit that he had made little headway with his murder enquiry. From what he told us it appeared that his gallery for interrogation almost exactly matched our own.

'Oh, and how are you getting on with that other little matter Mr Holmes . . . you know, the missing ring? I have heard rumours of a titled lady who lost valuable property yet made no official complaint.'

Holmes replied, 'Well Inspector, since you say no complaint has been made how can there be a loss? Come you are a stickler for officialdom?'

Lestrade winked and touched his nose, 'But we both know about it, do we not? Though I'll grant you, whatever I have heard, I cannot force a complaint. But I'll wager you know something about a very mysterious business!'

Holmes was saved from further cat and mouse activity by the interruption of Lestrade's plain clothes sergeant. He obviously wished to convey some information, yet hesitated due to our presence. Lestrade waved effusive hands and said, 'You may speak before Mr Holmes and Doctor Watson freely sergeant. Let us hope that in the future they will extend the same courtesy to us!'

'If you please sir, the old gent at the 'all, Mr Maskelyne,

'e says 'is 'orrible callipers 'as reappeared!'

I noticed that Lestrade consulted his notebook before he corrected his man. 'You mean his horologist's callipers!'

'Well gentlemen, shall we go to the Egyptian Hall and take a butchers at these callipers?' Holmes was unsurprised by the inspector's use of East End slang, saying, 'By all means, shall we take an "is as does" or a "ball and chalk"?' Lestrade looked puzzled. 'I know what a "ball and chalk" is, but an "is as does"?'

Holmes chuckled, 'Handsome is as handsome does! Surely you know the old adage Lestrade. I will lend you my monograph on London street argot. You might find it useful.' We took an 'is as does' to Maskelyne's.

The Grand Old Man of the Egyptian Hall received us affably enough; though he always appeared to have the look of a man with a secret to hide. Perhaps this was to be expected. However, he seemed ready enough to talk about the mysterious reappearance of his 'horologist's calliper'.

Holmes allowed Lestrade to examine the instrument first. I don't think the inspector was as interested in it as perhaps a policeman should have been considering it was a probable instrument of murder. He passed it to Holmes, saying, 'The distance between the teeth seems right, corresponding with the fingers on a hand. Beats me why whoever took it to do this grisly deed should have returned it. After all, some risk must have been incurred in doing so.'

Holmes said, 'At a quick guess I would say that whoever it was hoped that they would not have been missed. We can assume therefore, Mr Maskelyne, that the instrument is not in daily use?'

Maskelyne said, 'Quite so, it is used but once a week to wind the mechanism of my stenographic automata. One winding is enough for a number of performances.'

Lestrade asked, 'Might we trouble you to demonstrate the use of the calliper sir? I appreciate the secret nature of your apparatus and don't wish to pry into that . . . just the use of the instrument.'

Although Maskelyne replied, 'Quite so, of course!' I felt sure he was not absolutely delighted with the idea. Nevertheless, he cheerfully led the way to the spare room next to the fatal dressing room, where his automata was stored. He opened the lock with his complicated system, and threw open the door.

Lestrade asked if he could open the apparatus and show us the manner in which it was wound. Although Maskelyne did not ask us to stand well back, his attitude made us do so. He opened the door that revealed the giant 'clockwork', and applied the calliper so that it grasped a cog, the projections fitting the spaces between the cogs exactly. I could see that Holmes was fascinated, and not as unfamiliar with such arrangements as were the inspector and myself.

Holmes said, 'The mechanism is indeed beautifully made and although powerful is more subtle than that used in any of Houdin's automata.' Maskelyne mellowed a little and motioned Holmes to come closer to the apparatus. He quietly pointed out various points of interest in the machine's construction. Lestrade and I still stood back, feeling that the beckoning gesture had been meant for Holmes alone. The inspector met my gaze and the ghost of a smile played with the corners of his mouth. Then he gazed skywards for a few seconds.

We had retained the hansom, ordering its driver to await us at the theatre entrance. As we passed through the auditorium and into the lobby of the old theatre, David Devant appeared as if from nowhere. Maskelyne, obviously feeling his manager more than capable of performing the polite farewells, retreated, no doubt back to his eyrie.

'Mr Devant, Inspector . . .'

Holmes spoke as if inviting two co-conspiritors into some magic circle. 'May I ask you both to co-operate with me and give me your trust, for I believe that if you do, we can bring this terrible business to a just conclusion this very night.'

To say that I was amazed at the boldness of Holmes' prediction would be to put it mildly indeed.

He continued, 'Inspector, could you be here at the conclusion of tonight's performance with two or three discreetly placed constables? This is to prevent the departure of anyone connected with the entertainment.' Lestrade grunted, which I took to be a grudging assent. Holmes then turned to Devant and said, 'Mr Devant, we are both clear as to what is to happen, are we not?'

The conjurer nodded wisely and escorted us to the hansom. As we drove away from Piccadilly, Lestrade asked, drily and with a touch of sarcasm, 'Might I be permitted to know what this "something" you have arranged with Devant might be? I realise that I am only an Inspector of Detectives, but I do operate more efficiently when kept fully informed!'

Holmes chuckled, though not unkindly. 'Inspector we have been involved, you and I, in many an adventure. I believe I can safely say that to some extent Scotland Yard has benefited from our collusion?'

Lestrade coloured slightly, cleared his throat and then said, 'I believe I have once or twice had occasion to be grateful for your aid Mr Holmes. Indeed once or twice you have noticed some detail that has eluded me. But dash it all, a fellow likes to be kept informed.'

Holmes replied, 'This may be one of those occasions, like those you have mentioned where I have noticed some trifle that has eluded you. If you co-operate, as I have requested, you may make an arrest this very night.'

Lestrade said, 'You realise that you have no official place in any of this and my superiors will be furious if I waste time and resources.'

Holmes played a strong card. 'I don't think you will waste either and all kudos will be yours.'

I realised that my friend was dangling the fattest of maggots in front of a hungry roach. On reflection, perhaps a minnow in front of a pike is more apt. But certainly there was something fishlike about the way in which Lestrade opened and closed his mouth two or three times before he replied.

At last the inspector said, 'All right Mr Holmes, I'll go along with you. But this "something" of yours, whatever it is, had better work!'

Back at Baker Street I did not press Holmes for the details of his plan, which, if I understood him correctly, might solve the mystery surrounding poor Cyrano and see his killer apprehended in a matter of hours. He had told me very little more than he had told Lestrade. This I found a little hurtful, and I believe my manner toward my friend was a trifle cool.

Holmes said, 'There have been too many "breaking of silences"! You know Watson, there are times when I simply have to keep my own council. You see, even a trusted friend could unintentionally reveal some crumb of information, some mere trifle, but enough to put upon his guard the very person I least wish alerted.'

I understood, at least I thought I did, and I told him so. But I fear that I spoke without any great degree of conviction. Indeed, there could have been a touch of irony as I asked, 'Will you be wanting my company during your evening's adventure?'

Holmes chuckled at my remarks, though not unkindly. He said, 'Oh Watson, really, as if I could even contemplate embarking upon such an adventure without you. Before you think the worst of me, dear friend, I would like you to cast your mind back to that affair at Baskerville Hall, which by the way, I am surprised to note you have not yet bored your readers with! Do you remember that I sent you to Dartmoor, and led you to believe that I was still in London?'

I answered warmly, saying, 'I do indeed. You put me to the task of sending reports to you at Baker Street when unknown to me you were hidden out upon the moor, and living in a stone-age hut. I was furious when I discovered this fact!'

Holmes calmed me by saying, 'Your memory is short Watson, for I remember that I was able to explain to you at the time that I had excellent reasons for my eccentric behaviour. There were those upon the moor who I wished to be absolutely convinced that I was not upon the scene. You admitted to me later your acting ability would not have been up to the task had you known I was there.'

I had to agree that Holmes was right in his argument. Nonetheless I repeated my question.

Holmes replied, 'Indeed, I shall want you dressed and ready to depart for the Egyptian Hall at seven of the clock, stoutly shod and carrying your service revolver!'

I decided to take a late afternoon nap, leaving Holmes to his own devices. These consisted of perching himself upon the ottoman, producing clouds of acrid blue smoke from a meerscham full of the South African Differ-mixture.

I lay upon my bed and thought about all the adventures that Holmes and I had embarked upon during the dozen or so years of our association. I remembered the pain of believing he had died at the Reichenbach Falls. How time had passed, so very slowly and painfully for me until that unbelievable day in '94 when he had reappeared so dramatically. Since that day the clocks and calendars had again picked up momentum and life had again become rich, full and exciting. I remembered the fear of a year earlier that I might lose my friend when that savage nervous illness threatened to strike him down. My prayers for him had been answered, yet I could never admit to him that I, a doctor, had resorted to anything as unscientific as prayer.

It seemed to me that no sooner had I nodded off than the bedroom door flew open as if propelled by a hurricane. There, all but filling the height of the door aperture stood Holmes. I guessed that he had not rested, although he seemed fresh and alert. He was sedately dressed in evening clothes, complete with cape, cane and opera hat. He looked at me accusingly as he took a thin gold watch from his waistcoat. He consulted the timepiece, returned it to the pocket and said, very loudly indeed, 'Come Watson, stir yourself . . . The game's afoot!'

# CHAPTER EIGHT

# 'Grand Finale'

===================================================

The performance at the Egyptian Hall was becoming for me all but commonplace. After all, this was the third time that I had witnessed it within only a few days. It is said that 'familiarity breeds contempt', yet Holmes sat forward in his seat as if not wishing to miss a moment of the performance. The programme was much the same, except that Maskelyne dropped one of his plates, and De Kolta had added one or two new items to his act (at least, they were new to me). During the interval I mentioned to Holmes that the 'running-order' had again been altered, and this was the case in the second half of the performance, too. Maskelyne's son, Nevil, presented his mechanical secretary immediately before the 'Animated Photographs' which as usual brought the performance to its end.

As the curtain descended and the last notes of the national anthem died away, almost reluctantly the audience began to leave the theatre. They were happy with what they had seen and obviously considered it well worth the modest entrance fee. Although most of them had seen the moving pictures for the very first time, my eavesdropping revealed it was De Kolta's expanding cube that was the main point of conversation.

'How did it change in size?' and 'Where could she have come from?', these were the questions they asked each other as they poured out into Piccadilly. Their wonderment caused me to ponder: could this undoubted theatrical masterpiece be the cause of such a brutal murder . . . surely not? But perhaps I would soon know.

Holmes waved a hand, indicating that we should walk down the centre aisle toward the stage. He clapped his hands, and as if this were a theatrical 'cue', the heavy velvet curtains were raised. These revealed the members of the cast, seated about the stage in front of the large moving picture screen. Devant stood centre stage, as if about to give a performance. Several pieces of apparatus used in the performance were still in evidence, including the automata, which was stationed in one of the wings. J.N. Maskelyne stood near it, as if protecting his 'secret'. Cushions, stools, chairs from the dressing rooms, all had been brought into use for the cast and staff to be more or less comfortably seated. As we seated ourselves in the front stall seats, we were joined by Inspector Lestrade and his plain clothes sergeant.

Devant spoke up, as if addressing an audience, 'Mr Holmes, as you see, all is arranged as you requested. Now, our wish is your command!'

Holmes said, 'Inspector, Ladies and Gentlemen, I have asked you all to be here, that you might see Mr Devant's very latest animated picture, or "film" as he tells me such is termed. Mr Devant, if you please!'

Mr Devant clicked his fingers and the auditorium lights dimmed, whilst the still lighted projector started to throw an image upon the screen. The flickering picture could be clearly recognised as the exterior of Cyrano's dressing room window.

At this point Holmes gave Devant a 'signal', and the conjurer in turn signalled to the operator of the projector to stop the picture. On the screen all movement ceased, and there was just a giant picture of the exterior of the dressing room. Holmes said, so that all could hear him, 'You see before you a halted picture of the dressing room window, captured by Mr Devant on the night of the tragedy. The date can be established from the news-vender's board with its headline: "Kaiser bids for world peace!" Does anyone doubt that this film was taken on that day at that place?'

Lestrade spoke up, 'The board has been changed since and was different on the night before. Anyone can see that it is a picture of the outside of Cyrano's dressing room. But what is your point Mr Holmes, save that someone took this er . . . film, on that particular night? Oh yes, and night it is, you can tell by the light, which seems to come only from that lamp-post to the right in the picture.'

Holmes said, 'Just have a little patience Inspector. Mr Devant, if you please!'

The picture recommenced its flickering and as the window was seen to open a little, the figure of a man could be seen through it. As his head fully emerged, everyone gasped, 'It's Craig, Matthew Craig!' As the figure clambered out with difficulty and hurried from the scene there could be little doubt. The picture flickered to its finish.

Lestrade leapt onto the stage and walked toward the bemused Matthew Craig, who blurted, 'All right, I can't deny it now! That is me undoubtedly as you can all see. But how, and why were you filming that window Mr Devant?'

The inspector said, 'Never mind that for now, you admit, before all these people that the . . . er . . . image, is of yourself, and you agree that it must have been taken on the night of the murder?'

'Yes, yes, I've said so . . . what else can I do?' The Illusionist's helper had been shocked into a blurted confession and could see no way out of it. Lestrade laid a hand on his shoulder, saying, 'Matthew Craig, I hereby arrest you for the murder of one Cyril Raymond, also known as Cyrano. I must caution you . . .'

Lestrade got no further in his official 'caution', because Holmes rose from his seat and walked the four small steps onto the stage. He raised a hand, stopping the flow of the police inspector's words. Craig took advantage of this momentary silence to blurt out, 'I didn't murder Cyrano, the blighter was dead when I got to his dressing room!'

At this point Holmes 'took the stage' . . .

'Inspector, what you have heard is true. All you can arrest Craig for is the theft of a diamond ring, and the probable theft of the plans, belonging to Mr De Kolta, for his expanding cube illusion!'

At this news De Kolta launched into a furious speech and would have exploded into violent action had he not been restrained by Nevil Maskelyne and David Devant.

Holmes continued, 'I deduced that Craig had given Cyrano the plans on the promise that when the illusion was produced he would receive a large sum of money . . .' He was interrupted by Craig, who shouted, 'The blighter said he'd give me five hundred pounds, then when I got there he was dead. I searched everywhere for the money. I was desperate: Mr De Kolta was sure to find out. I wanted to get out of town. All I could find was a diamond ring in a trick box. I sold the ring and was going to go to Scotland, but when De Kolta got the engagement for the Egyptian

Hall he seemed to forget that Cyrano had the secret. Cyrano was dead and could not tell, so I decided to risk it and stay.'

Holmes had allowed Craig his say, because it suited his purpose. Now he continued. 'I suspected Craig's involvement for a number of reasons. He appeared with Cyrano in old fairground photographs, and I knew that he was as lithe as I, and could climb through an aperture too small to admit most other suspects. I secretly arranged with Mr Devant to make a "film", in which I impersonated Craig, aided by a wig and some theatrical make-up. You may remember Watson we remarked on Craig's unusual quiff. I am not without practice in theatrical disguise. The matter of the news-vender's placard was not difficult to arrange, for a half-crown tip. Just think how many newspapers one must sell to get thirty pence! Now, is there anything not yet explained?'

I could not restrain myself from asking, 'But Holmes, if these facts are as you say they are, and Craig is not the murderer, why did you go to such an amount of trouble to produce this charade, and put Mr Devant to such enormous trouble in filming this scene and producing a positive version of it in record time?'

Holmes was almost apologetic, almost, though not quite. He answered, 'At the time when I collaborated with Mr Devant to produce what you have seen I believed Mr Craig to be the murderer. It was only quite recently that I became sure that he was not.'

Lestrade was almost apoplectic at this statement, rounding on Holmes with, 'See here Holmes, you have brought me here with police resources knowing that this clever demonstation could only convict a man of robbery or so you say! My brief is to catch a murderer. Well, I'm not too sure that this man Craig is not still a suspect. I've a mind to arrest him and confiscate the film for evidence. I have to show my superiors something to justify time and expense!'

Holmes said, 'But Inspector, would not your superiors be even more grateful if you were to produce the real murderer?'

Even I thought that Holmes was pushing his luck with Lestrade. After all, although brilliant, the demonstration had not really done anything for the inspector, apart from gaining his irate attention.

Like a conjurer threatening to produce a rabbit, Holmes asked, 'Lestrade, I told you that you might make your arrest this night, but the night is not over yet. Bear with me and if I am right in my deductions, you may have your murderer. At the time when I all but promised you your arrest, earlier today, I was already sure in my mind that Craig was innocent of all save robbery. It was not he that I thought of . . .'

'Oh . . .' said Lestrade now obviously anxious to placate the Baker Street detective. 'Are you telling me you know who it is?'

'I think I know and I'm seldom wrong . . . Watson will verify that.' Lestrade was very impatient, 'Mr Holmes, *please!*'

My friend began a story of amazing accusation which would astonish every one of us.

'I began to be intrigued by the fact that the closets in the Cyrano dressing room and the empty one next door used only for storage, had some kind of linking door, of a simple enough kind. I did not at that time wish it known that I knew of its existence, and I was never alone in the room to examine this arrangement as closely as I would have liked. Its actuality was borne out by back stage stories of ghostly voices seeming at times to come from the locked room. Its window, unlike that in Cyrano's room, was barred, no doubt on account of the secret nature of the items stored therein.'

Lestrade was impatient, 'You mean the killer entered Cyrano's room through a secret door linking the two cupboards?'

Holmes bowed slightly, 'Bear with me Lestrade, I come now to the means of the killing, effected with Mr Maskelyne's winding calliper. This means of attack suggests that we need no longer look only for a strongly built or large person. I remembered the photograph of the midget troupe, in Cyrano's album. Also, backstage gossip suggested that Cyrano had been extremely unpleasant to one of these midgets.'

I asked, 'But was there anywhere in the room where even a midget could hide himself Holmes?'

'Not so far as I could see at the time.'

'Then . . .'

Holmes continued, 'I took the photograph to a theatrical agent in the King's Cross area. He was able to identify one of the midgets and gave his name as Kurt Schmidtt, as well as the name of another agent who sometimes obtained bookings for him.'

Then Holmes dropped his 'bombshell' which brought Lestrade, who had settled on a stool, to his feet.

'This second agent told me that he had recently obtained a booking for Kurt Schmidtt with J.N. Maskelyne, at the Egyptian Hall.'

'What?' Lestrade was alert now, 'That's too much of a coincidence!'

'My very own feeling Lestrade, yet no midget appears on the programme presented at this theatre.'

The Inspector walked over to where the Grand Old Man of the Egyptian Hall stood next to his automata. 'Mr

Maskelyne, is this true . . . did you in fact engage this midget, and if so, why have we not seen him?'

J.N. Maskelyne suddenly looked rather old. He said, 'Inspector, I did indeed engage a midget, but as you can see he does not appear to be here.' His son, Neil, intervened. 'Please Inspector, my father is not a young man and must not become excited, due to his heart.'

'But man, I have to know!'

Holmes took on the 'starring role' again, 'Inspector, I believe I can save both Messrs Maskelyne further grief by explaining what I believe to be the truth.'

Lestrade pleaded, 'Please, *please* do!'

'Due to Mr Maskelyne's secrecy, my examination of the automata, stored in the spare dressing room was of a cursory nature. Even so, I could see that the portion housing the clockwork mechanism was rather large. In any case I could not believe that a simple clockwork mechanism such as it was, could perform such a sophisticated job. Even before I identified Schmidtt I had started to believe that a small person, perhaps even a child, must be hidden behind the mechanism in order to operate a duplicate set of typing keys, connected to the letters themselves by leads. Of course I realised that the model "secretary" was a bit of showman's sham, and eventually that the clockwork was also!

'Then the business of the missing and reappearing winding calliper came into the picture, and its identification as a murder weapon. Its real use was for the occasional winding of the sham clockwork, in order that it would move and give the impression required. Everything started to fall together in my mind. Through his mania for secrecy Mr Maskelyne found it necessary to regularly smuggle the midget out of the apparatus and out of the room via the secret door linking the two closets. This meant that when everyone but he had left the theatre, Mr Maskelyne could allow his midget a few hours of freedom, and therefore had no need to disturb the complicated locks. The lock to Cyrano's dressing room could be opened with a schoolboy's penknife, but no one would think to try and get to the secret room that way. Whatever his grudge, once he had realised that Cyrano was in the room next to him, he could not resist planning to kill him and carrying out that plan. When Maskelyne took him into his eyrie, he managed to annex the calliper and returned it later.'

The Old Man interceded, 'I trusted him, and even let him eat late night meals with me in the attic!'

Holmes concluded, 'I may have missed some small details, but that I believe is the true picture of what happened.'

Nevil Maskelyne was the next to speak. 'Very astute of you Mr Holmes, and you refer to my father's mania for secrecy. But had you seen how he has suffered at the hands of "pirates", as indeed has Mr De Kolta, you would perhaps not think too harshly of him over this affair.'

Lestrade said, 'And I suppose this Schmidtt has got clean away whilst we have been listening to all this?'

Sherlock Holmes said, 'On the contrary Lestrade. Through a special arrangement between myself and Mr Devant the automata has remained in the wings since it was used in the performance. I believe that you will find Kurt Schmidt to be still inside.'

Lestrade looked at the machine in disbelief. He said, 'I'll believe that there is a man in there when I see him step out of it. Anyone can see that the mannikin on top is worked by clockwork!'

He swung the door on the apparatus open to bare the mechanism to our gaze. I had to admit that there did not appear to be anywhere to conceal a man, however small.

Then quite suddenly, like an inner door, that wall of mechanics swung open, bearing out Holmes' theory. From the compartment thus revealed, there stepped one of the smallest men that I have ever seen. It was difficult to gauge his age, but he was perfectly proportioned: in other words not a dwarf. His height appeared to be about three feet. He had close cropped hair and a fiercely waxed moustache of the type sported by the German Kaiser. He spoke in a high, clear voice, with a distinct German accent.

'Gentlemens, I believe you are looking for me? My name is Kurt Schmidt and I am a subject of his Majesty, the Kaiser Wilhelm. I have heard all that you have been saying, and I wish you to know Mr Holmes that you are absolutely right in almost all your deductions concerning my actions. I had vowed that one day I would kill Cyrano. My chance came, and I took it. It was not easy to do, even with the geared calliper, but I was able to trip him, and once on the floor he had no chance.'

Holmes looked at the strange little man sternly yet not without compassion and asked, 'My deductions regarding your motive were correct then?'

'Yes, he was not merely unpleasant to me in Vienna, but he actually did me great harm. The worst thing he did to me was to secretly shorten my walking cane, and replace the ferrule. This made me believe that I was growing taller.'

I said quite the wrong thing. 'But surely, you would want to have been taller?'

He said, 'Herr Doctor, you do not understand theatrical things and the world of the show grounds. Twenty five years ago I would have given anything to be taller. But once I had come to terms with my tragedy and realised that I could capitalise on it, my feelings were quite

different. My height is actually thirty-seven inches. I have
known other men as small as myself who started to grow,
in their twenties or even thirties. Not more than perhaps
eight inches or so, but enough to make them useless for
show business. After all, who would want a four foot
midget? He is neither fish nor fowl.'

Holmes asked, 'It was an *affaire de cour* was it not?' I
thought it a misplaced joke on Holmes' part, but the
midget nodded his head.

'Yes, of a sort. Cyrano's lady partner, Madame Patricia,
was always very kind to me. But Cyrano, who was a
foolish man, as well as an evil one, misunderstood, and
thought that he must do me harm . . .'

The lady in question had been standing well back, a
hand covering the astonishment of her mouth. Now she
ran forward and laid a kindly hand upon the little man's
shoulder. She spoke to him, 'My little friend, I had no idea
that he had tried to harm you. I just thought that you were
sick.'

Schmidtt placed a small hand upon hers and said, 'I
know dear lady, you were always kind. Well, I was sick,
sick with worry at my supposed increase in height. When
it got round the fairground that I believed I was growing,
everyone said to me, "Why Kurt, you look bigger . . . I'm
sure you are growing." But I realise now that there was no
evil in them, just in Cyrano. My work started to suffer,
and I started to become a secret drinker. I ruined one
acrobatic trick too many and lost my employment.'

I asked, 'What did you do then?'

He said, 'I obtained work, very low paid, as a midget
clown in a circus. The sort of work that a midget that had
actually grown might find. Then, after about a year I had
an accident, and fell on my head. I landed in hospital
where I was given a very thorough examination. The

doctor was very interested in me. I suppose it was not every day he had the chance to examine a midget. He even measured me, and discovered that I was exactly thirty-seven inches tall! After that there came a change in my fortunes, despite which I still planned that I would kill Cyrano some day, just for the hell that he had put me through. When I heard that he was in England I came here and worked for a time for "Lord" George Sanger. When Cyrano started at this theatre I came to London. Then, when I heard that Herr Maskelyne was looking for a "secret little man" I knew that my chance had come. Had it not been for the Great Sherlock Holmes I believe that the traitor, Craig, would have paid for my crime, as well as his own.'

Holmes nodded curtly and said, 'That might seem just to you Herr Schmidtt, but in Britain, truth and justice are paramount.'

Schmidtt said, 'But it will not be in a British courtroom that this matter will be tried, at least as far as I am concerned. As a German citizen I believe I can demand to be deported. In Germany they have a rather different outlook upon a matter of this kind.'

Lestrade, who had seemed to be in a trancelike state, suddenly sprang to life. He gave a signal to bring the hurried appearance of one of his constables. Then he glared sternly down at the midget and said, 'Kurt Schmidtt, I hereby arrest you for the murder of one Cyril Randolph, professionally known as Cyrano . . .'

'I protest, I am a subject of the Kaiser!'

'That might be, young fellow-me-lad, but for the moment you are my prisoner and anything you say may be used in evidence . . .'

This time the inspector had the right man.

As for Matthew Craig, he was remarkably fortunate. Not only was he cleared of the murder, but he was actually forgiven his disloyalty by his employer, Buatier De Kolta, who stated that the fault could have been his own through not paying Craig enough. This, he said, was something he would rectify.

On our return to Baker Street, over a nightcap, I remarked to Holmes upon De Kolta's extreme docility in the matter.

'I cannot help but remember that wild man who frenziedly shouted dire threats at Cyrano, when he presented that very illusion which has become so much a bone of contention. Now, instead of wanting to kill Craig he raises his pay!'

Holmes said, 'How very Hungarian Watson! De Kolta is more Hungarian than French.'

On the day following, Holmes sent for Matthew Craig to come to 221b. The detective was stern in his manner toward him.

'You must realise Craig that you have only your own dishonesty and irresponsible actions to blame for the fact that you came within a whisper of being arrested, accused of a capital offence?'

Very much 'cap in hand', Craig said, 'Yes, I have only myself to blame. What have you decided about that little matter of the diamond ring Mr Holmes?'

My friend started. 'Little matter . . . you call the theft of what you took to be a very valuable trinket a "little matter"?'

'Perhaps I expressed myself badly . . .'

'You did! Now listen to me carefully Craig. I believe that if you follow my advice, to the letter, you need not fear police involvement.'

'Please tell me what I must do sir, your wish is my command.'

My friend winced at the sickly phrase, and said, 'Well to begin with, you will never trouble the owner of the ring. It has been returned to her, and that is the last that need concern her. To continue, only one person has actually suffered through the theft, Stringer, the jeweller, who paid you a large sum of money for it.'

'But . . . but he's just a fence!'

Holmes rounded on him sharply, 'Exactly, and you are just a thief!'

Craig lowered his head in either real or assumed shame. He said, very quietly, 'What then is your guidance?'

Sherlock Holmes tamped the tobacco in his clay pipe. Prior to lighting it, he asked, 'Do you still have the money that he paid you, or have you already spent all or part of it?'

'I have spent none of it, I have it all.'

'Very well then, you will go to Stringer and repay him. Rest assured I will hear of it if you don't. After that you can forget the affair, always assuming your future life is blameless. Should you stray from the straight and narrow path in the future, especially in your dealings with your employer, I will be forced to bring every one of your dishonest details to the attention of the authorities. While Inspector Lestrade is too interested in his murder to pay much attention to you, there are other persons who would be fascinated with the details of your activities.'

After Craig had left us, Holmes said to me, 'You know Watson, Lady Windrush has also emerged fortunate from this affair, though I admit that her continued good fortune will depend upon the behaviour of Craig. I do not anticipate any problems from his direction.'

I said, 'Then she is lucky indeed.'

Holmes came the nearest I have ever seen to a wink, short of that action. He said to me, 'The good lady is lucky indeed to have such a good friend as Doctor John Watson!'

I didn't quite know how to reply.

The following day we had a visit from Inspector Lestrade of Scotland Yard. I wondered if he would compliment Holmes upon the investigation, demonstration and deductions which had enabled him to make his arrest. He appeared to be a little sheepish and unsure of what his stance should be. But Holmes, whilst not exactly putting Lestrade at his ease, broke the ice as far as conversation was concerned.

He said, 'Ah, Inspector, I congratulate you upon your acceptance into the ranks of "The Knights of Alchemy". I do not approve much of secret societies myself, but I'm sure that membership will have its advantages for you.'

Lestrade growled, 'Really Mr Holmes, a body can't do anything without you getting to hear of it. Who told you, my sergeant?'

Holmes threw back his head in honest laughter. He turned to me and said, 'A bulls-eye Watson!' Then turning to Lestrade he said, 'Nobody told me — I was in ignorance of your membership until you stepped into this room.'

'Then how . . .'

'Oh come Inspector, it is a little early in the year for salt-water paddling, and in any case for that activity *both* trouser legs are rolled to the knee. Simple observation shows me that just one leg of your usually immaculate nether garment has been recently rolled to the knee. I am aware that such rolling of a trouser leg is part of the ritual involved in the membership ceremony. A little childish I think.'

Lestrade said, glumly, 'If you want to get into the really

high ranks in my profession Mr Holmes, you have to be a member.'

More seriously, Holmes said, 'I am aware of that, I have written a monograph upon the subject of "Secret Societies and the Ruling Establishment".'

With the air of one with a painful duty to perform Lestrade said, 'Very interesting, but I just came to say that I'm grateful to you for saving me the indignity of arresting the wrong man, and, I think I have mentioned before, that on occasion you have noticed some details that I have overlooked. As I say, I'm grateful for your co-operation.'

He had said it all in one breath like a child delivering a compulsory recitation.

Holmes, as always, received this gratitude with grace, saying, 'Not at all Lestrade, it was not our first collusion, nor our last I'll be bound. But tell me, shall you have to surrender your prisoner, Kurt Schmidtt to the German authorities?'

Lestrade looked smug. He said, 'No sir, I shall not!' but he did not enlarge upon this.

I said, 'But surely Lestrade, as a subject of the Kaiser, deportation is his right? He is sure to elect for that course, as I believe he might get a more lenient treatment in his own country. You know on the continent they look upon these things rather differently, especially if there is even the slightest hint of an *affaire de cour* involved!'

Lestrade answered, 'That may or may not be so, and may or may not be right. Certainly the foreigners have some quaint ways of interpreting their laws. But rest assured, Kurt Schmidtt will be tried in a proper English court room, with a proper English judge and jury. More-over, he will undoubtedly hang! Our juries take a poor view of people being choked to death, even with a horology calliper and by a three foot high man!'

Holmes was intrigued, 'How have you managed to hold onto him Lestrade?'

'How, ah yes. He is no more a German than I am a Dutchman. He *was* a German, but some months ago he put in for citizenship papers. It's just his bad luck that his citizenship has just been granted. I say "just", because he was not even aware that the papers had gone through until I told him!'

Holmes whistled, 'Phew! I never thought I would live to see a day when I was sorry for a fellow for becoming British! I say though Inspector, isn't there anything we can do for the little chap? The circumstances are rather unusual.'

Lestrade shrugged. 'The law must be upheld Mr Holmes, the law must be upheld.'

Holmes nodded grimly, saying, 'You are right Inspector. But I cannot help thinking that a thirty seven inch man, having avenged himself, hardly constitutes a danger to the rest of the population.'

Kurt Schmidtt was a remarkable man. Not only was he a mere three foot and one inch tall, but he was probably the smallest man to be tried in England for the crime of murder, and certainly the smallest to be hung.

Some weeks later a package arrived at the Baker Street rooms, addressed in perfect copperplate to 'Sherlock Holmes, Esq.' We did not play our usual game but rather hastily the detective removed the wrappings with an impatience that said to me, 'Watson . . . no deductions . . . by request' just as surely as if he had spoken. A framed print of the Egyptian Hall edifice as it had been perhaps some fifty years earlier was revealed. An enclosed card bore the penned message, 'With the Compliments and thanks of Maskelyne and Devant.' Holmes said, 'From the latter rather than the former I fancy. Maskelyne is a gentleman who has strayed upon the stage and in his heart abhors sensational publicity. Devant is a theatrical who has strayed into society and adores it!'

Holmes was correct of course and not long afterwards I received a letter from the elder Maskelyne, informing me that he would deem it a personal favour if I would refrain from including the details of our Egyptian Hall adventure in my series of 'The Strand' magazine narratives. He wrote, 'Of course the more sensational journalists have had a field day already. But I implore you not to bring the matter back to the public mind through one of your pieces.'

I could only agree to refrain from using that which would have made such an excellent exploit or adventure. However, now that some thirty years have passed, I see no reason to keep the facts from my readers any longer. J.N. Maskelyne died in 1917 and Devant is a helpless cripple in a bathchair. The Egyptian Hall has long been demolished and as for my friend Mr Sherlock Holmes, some time ago he exchanged his silk hat and morning-dress for a panama and an alpaca jacket, and tends his bees on the Sussex Downs.